W9-CTS-832

FAYE KAY
9408 143 ST NW
EDMONTON AB
T5R 0P7

CANADA

THE DIALOGUES OF TIME

AND ENTROPY

THE DIALOGUES OF TIME

AND ENTROPY

Aryeh Lev Stollman

Riverhead Books

a member of Penguin Putnam Inc.

New York 2003

These stories, some in slightly different form, were originally published in the following journals and magazines: "Die Grosse Liebe" in *The Yale Review*; "The Creation of Anat," "The Seat of Higher Consciousness," and "The Dialogues of Time and Entropy" in *American Short Fiction*; "The Little Poet" in *Story*; "Mr. Mitochondria" in *Pakn Treger*; "The Adornment of Days" in *Southwest Review*; "Enfleurage" in *Puerto del Sol*; "If I Have Found Favor in Your Eyes" in *Tikkun*; "New Memories" in *The Fiddlehead*.

Riverhead Books
a member of
Penguin Putnam Inc.
375 Hudson Street
New York, NY 10014

Library of Congress Cataloging-in-Publication Data

Stollman, Aryeh Lev.
The dialogues of time and entropy / Aryeh Lev Stollman.
p. cm.
Contents: Die grosse Liebe—The adornment of days—
The creation of Anat—Mr. Mitochondria—If I have found
favor in your eyes—Enfleurage—The seat of higher
consciousness—The little poet—New memories—
The dialogues of time and entropy.
ISBN 1-57322-235-6
I. Jews—Fiction 2. Mind and body—Fiction. I.Title.
PS3569.T6228 D53 2003   2002068269
813'.54—dc21

Printed in the United States of America
1 3 5 7 9 10 8 6 4 2

This book is printed on acid-free paper. ∞

Book design by Meighan Cavanaugh

For

Henriette Simon Picker

and for

Tobias Picker

CONTENTS

Mr. Mitochondria

Enfleurage

Die Grosse Liebe

The Adornment of Days

New Memories

MR. MITOCHONDRIA

❧   ❧   ❧

We were having breakfast on the spring day before the locusts arrived. My family lived on the outskirts of Beersheba in
one of those large white boxlike structures that bloomed in
the sands of the Negev in the fifties and sixties. My parents,
emigrants from Canada, had lovingly planted the yard with
flowering succulents, brilliant desert varieties that filled their
winter-bred souls with wonder and upon which they bestowed
allegorical names. Outside the kitchen lay heavy rolls of transparent plastic between the purple pinnacles of Sarah's Handmaiden and the waxy crimson blossoms of Job's Wife. For the
last several days, the radio and newspapers were full of terrifying reports on the desert grasshopper, "the largest infestation

of the century," swarming over the Arabian Peninsula to the east, and ready to migrate across the Red Sea.

Adar, nine at the time, had spent several afternoons after school drawing all the plants in his sketchbook "so when they get killed, we can remember them." When he said this, Mother covered her ears with her hands. "Oh, God, please don't be so morbid. They're my special babies! I couldn't bear to lose a single one." Under each meticulous depiction of fleshy trunk, flower, and seed, Adar wrote the species' Latin name. To the side he drew a hovering, glowering figure, six-winged and brandishing a fiery staff—the threatened plant's guardian angel. "See, Tishrei," Adar said, pointing to one of the figures, "they all have curly red hair like you."

That morning, as usual, Father was preoccupied with his whole-grain cereal, weighing exactly 55 grams, 180 calories, of organically grown cracked wheat and bulgur, and measuring exactly 250 milliliters of nonfat milk, 9.2 grams of protein. Father, who had always been perfectly healthy and lean, had recently begun to mistrust the innate brilliance of human physiology. He now stood guard against its errors, discounting the experience of his own well-functioning kidneys in keeping his bodily fluids and electrolytes balanced, or the wisdom of his liver and pancreas to metabolize the varying amounts and types of amino acids and sugars that a normal person might chance to take in from day to day. "Honey, you really ought to try and have more faith," Mother would say. "Faith keeps our atoms from flying apart and has restored us in this wilderness." Father answered with a half-smile, "Kayla, I have faith, but it's not an antidote to reality."

Mr. Mitochondria

That morning as Adar came into the kitchen, Father put down the graduated cup he used to measure his milk. Adar looked less like a child than like a miniature man, a small, skinny replica of our father with the same smooth black hair and the same pale gray eyes. "Alien eyes," Mother called them, "windows to the alien soul."

"Well, Adar, I had a chance to read your report last night." Father held up the draft of Adar's entry into the National Science Institute's contest for schoolchildren. "It's outstanding. And your research proposal is brilliant. After all, imagination is the secret to all great discoveries. You're going to win." After a long pause Father continued solemnly, "I'm proud of you, Adar. You're a prodigy."

"A prodigy? Where? In my kitchen?" Mother, in a narrow white caftan and sandals, stood by the stove, her red hair tied in a long ponytail. After moving to the desert Mother still practiced the cuisine of her snowy Toronto childhood. Holding a skillet, she flipped a blueberry pancake high into the air, her intense gaze never leaving the revolving spotted disc. "A prodigy? That's quite a heavy label!" Adar was hurt at this implied negation of his new status. He stared at his lap. The pancake completed its brief parabolic flight and landed in the skillet, raw side down, with a faint sizzle.

Mother, eventually, if not instantly, sensitive to the effects of her words, made a clumsy retreat. "Of course, he's prodigiously smart." She slid the pancake onto Adar's dish. "The women of the planet Ichalob are extremely jealous of me"—Mother had been working on her epic trilogy, *The Ichalob Chronicles*—"despite the fact that the mothers are preoccupied, what with all the

3

upsetting prophecies emanating from their moons, and their children being killed fighting the Uranites. Well, no matter what anyone says, I wouldn't trade in my children for all the particle transformers in Galaxy Five."

Father looked at her, alarmed. "What are you talking about?"

"Talking about? The particle transformers? It's just something I made up."

Father took a long breath, looked at us with his pale gray eyes, the eyes that Adar shared. "What I was trying to say, Kayla, is that you should not dismiss the fact that Adar might be more than *very smart*. The boy has something extra in him. An undeveloped, an *unconventional* genius. I don't know why I overlooked this before. He sees things differently. It should be encouraged."

Mother rolled her eyes, then leaned over Adar. "Why aren't you eating your pancake?"

"I can't. It's made with squished insects. Their purple blood is leaking out."

"You've eaten plenty of blueberries in plenty of pancakes before."

"I'm fasting so the locusts won't come."

Mother took away Adar's plate. "Well, I suppose we should all be fasting as the people of Nineveh did, or Queen Esther when trouble was brewing. God does appreciate a fast, but I have the feeling it's already too late and the locusts will eat everything and you'll be starving to death."

⚓

My brother and I were named for the lunar months in which we were born: Tishrei, the autumn month when the world was created and is repeatedly judged, and Adar, the last month of the rainy season, when God is especially gracious to His People, the month before Spring waves her fertile wand across the land.

Adar was clearly very smart, but to be a real live prodigy one had to accomplish some incredible feat at an extremely young, postfetal age. Like the Sage of Vilna, who as an infant recited the correct blessing for milk at his mother's breast. That was a prodigy. Or John Stuart Mill, who read the Greek classics at three. Adar was no John Stuart Mill. He was no little Mozart composing *Eine Kleine Nachtmusik.*

Father was a researcher at an experimental nuclear station in the desert. Mother often told the story of their "great migration" from Canada to this faraway and unlikely scientific outpost. While Father was still a postdoctoral fellow in Toronto and already married to Mother, he wrote his first monograph, *Theoretical Deuterium Fusion in Enhanced Magnetic Fields.* Soon after its publication, he was approached by emissaries from the Negev Nuclear Authority, who were scouting the world for new scientific talent.

"They courted your father more persistently and, I might add, more romantically than he courted me. They made extravagant predictions, 'You will help shape the destiny of your people and ensure the survival of their children.' And they made a wonderful promise, music to any scientist's ears: 'You can do whatever research you want.' They took both of us on a secret trip halfway across the world to see the desert and the facility, to help us think things over. I was still very sad then, and I suddenly felt like I had traveled to another planet. That's when I had my first vision of Ichalob. And I understood even then that despite appearances, Ichalob was not a lifeless world. You know, it had very lush botanical life during its watery epoch that endured into the imperial desert age as well. But anyway it was a good thing that I became so inspired to write my trilogy, because otherwise I would have gone crazy."

Father rarely discussed his work, and when he did, only in the vaguest terms. "I'm working hard on this new project," or, "My experiments are going very well," he might tell Mother on those frequent nights when he came home late. We were led to understand that Father's work was very important and of a secret, restricted nature. Sometimes we were allowed to visit him at the low-rise outer buildings of the research facility. There he had an office filled with bulky computer equipment and large blackboards covered with the endless and incomprehensible chatter of equations. We were never allowed in the domed complex that housed the nuclear reactor. "I'm sorry, I'd like to but it's not a tourist attraction."

In contrast to the secretive Negev Nuclear Authority, the National Science Institute was open to the public and a source of great pride and prestige to the country. The Institute, with its yearly contest, sought to encourage creative thinking from schoolchildren in the realm of research. Adar's entry, "Mitochondria, the Powerhouses of the Cell: How We Should Study Them Better," was, per the contest instructions, part science report and part proposal for innovative research. Mitochondria, the microscopic organelles that dwell within all living cells, are, in reality, ancient bacteria, tiny specks of life that invaded our ancestral cells and made their home there. In exchange for lodging, they provide energy for life processes. Father acted as if Adar had discovered mitochondria himself instead of having gleaned known facts from the encyclopedia and the many scientific journals and magazines that filled huge bookcases throughout our house. Adar, in his own words, had proposed an original avenue for cellular research that impressed Father, and, as it turned out, the National Science Institute as well: "We should study the mitochondria of the locusts that are coming, because they travel very far and need lots of energy, so they must have many mitochondria. It would be like a human person walking a million miles after eating only a sandwich. It may be important to wear gloves when touching the insects in case they are poisonous or have contagious and fatal diseases." Adar submitted several drawings of a migratory locust he had copied from the encyclopedia with small arrows pointing to the hypermetabolic wing muscles.

"You know, Tishrei," Adar said in the bedroom the night of his elevation to prodigyhood, the night before the locusts arrived, "it's creepy to think we have these parasites in our cells and would die without them. Maybe someone could destroy the mitochondria in the locusts and they would all die." There was a faint and nervous quaver in his voice. "And you know what else, Tishrei? You only inherit them from your mother, never your father. Mitochondria have their own separate DNA."

"How do you know? Did you ever see one? It's just a theory."

"It's not a theory, Tishrei. It's a scientific fact. I read it."

"It's a sci-en-tif-ic faaact! It's a sci-en-tif-ic faaact! I read it! I read it! 'I'm so smart! I'm a prodigy!'"

Adar was on the verge of tears. "Don't be jealous, Tishrei. I never said that. You're two years older. You're smarter than me."

Just then Mother, the source of all our mitochondria, came into the room. "What's going on? I thought I heard talking!"

"Hi, Mom," Adar said, trying to sound calm.

Mother walked toward the window. "Why aren't you asleep? Are you too hot? It's already cool outside, so I've turned off the air-conditioner. I'll open this window some more. Tomorrow we have to get up extra early—we have a lot of work to do." She hesitated at the doorway. "You know, maybe we should read something together to prepare us." She came back a moment later and began reading from the Book of Yo'el. "'That which the cutting locust has left, the swarming locust has eaten; and that which the hopping locust has left, the destroying locust has eaten.'"

Adar suddenly grabbed her arm. "Mom, please stop reading. I'm tired."

"Oh, I'm sorry. You must be exhausted."

She stayed awhile longer to say the bedtime prayers: "On my right is Michoel, on my left Gavriel, before me Uriel, and behind me Refael."

After she left the room Adar called out softly as he always did when he was very frightened, "Tishrei, look at me. Okay? Watch me until I fall asleep. Okay? Please."

Next morning our father woke everyone up before sunrise. "Mother Nature is on the march!"

On the radio we heard that the locusts had begun crossing the Red Sea at twenty kilometers per hour. Schools were closed in the southern half of the country and the population was urged to remain indoors. The air force was on alert, ready to spray the invading clouds of insects with tons of insecticides. The radio explained how the pilots would have to fly around and then above the swarms in order to avoid clogging their engines with locusts. The government warned that the spraying would only decrease but not eliminate the terrible pest. At first Adar would not come out of the house until Father reassured him that the locusts would not arrive for several hours. In the cool dawn light Mother handed out kerchiefs to wear around our mouths and noses to prevent inhalation of the insecticides, even though the spraying had not yet begun. We looked like bandits from a western. We placed dozens of tall metal stakes at equal intervals in the ground, and Father hammered them in for supports. We spread the thin, clear plastic above the plants, tying the edges of the material to the stakes with string. The yard resembled a great tabernacle.

"It's like a wedding canopy for plants," Father said, taking hold of Mother. They drew close and danced awkwardly for a few moments, brushing against the covered blue flowers of Joseph Is Not. Mother began singing "The Voice of the Bridegroom, the Voice of the Bride." Father laughed. I thought Mother was laughing, too, but then I realized she had begun crying. She seemed to me as delicate and vulnerable as any of the wonders in our garden. Father broke off from dancing. He smoothed her hair back from her face. "Everything will be fine, Kayla. Like you say, we need to have faith. We'd better finish now. I almost knocked something over. And I still have to go to the lab."

Mother had stopped crying. "You shouldn't have to be driving in the open today with them spraying chemicals. You should be indoors. You're the one who's become so health-conscious."

"I'm in the middle of a project. I can't just stop. Besides, I'm sorry to inform you, all these precautions are useless. They'll be spraying the stuff for miles and way up in the air. It will be everywhere. Like strontium 90."

Adar turned pale. He pulled the fingers of one small hand with the other. "Is there really strontium 90 in this desert? I thought it was only in America. It gives you cancer and makes your bones fall apart!"

"I was just kidding. Don't worry."

"What about all the insect poisons, Dad? They're nerve poisons, aren't they? Mom says——"

"You and your mother worry too much. The spray quickly dissipates. The wind will blow it all out to sea in a day."

Father began walking toward the car, removing the kerchief from his face.

After Father drove off, we went indoors. "'Worry too much!'" Mother said. "As if I didn't have reason. If I had better sense and hadn't been so preoccupied with the goings-on on Ichalob, I would have taken us back to Toronto until this plague was over! Well, maybe I'll get some new ideas for *The Ichalob Chronicles.*"

Mother went haphazardly around the house, closing windows. "Please, leave them shut. I don't want any contaminated air in here. I don't want to be poisoned."

"We'll run out of oxygen!" Adar said. Even though we were indoors, he would not take his kerchief off his mouth and nose.

"Don't be silly. Besides, we can still leave the central air-conditioning on. It has a new filter. Now I'd better get some real work done. The slave Queen of Ichalob and her retinue are in secret revolt against the evil King and have declared a solemn fast to ensure its success. They are going to destroy the particle transformer by releasing millions of scientifically created pseudoseraphs from their force-field clouds. The children must be saved!" As she closed her writing room door behind her we could still hear her: "Yes, thank God, *all* the children will be saved."

Adar went to his desk and looked over his drawings of the garden plants with their Latin names and their guardian angels. He fussed over each and every one of them, adding some details here, a bit of color there. He even drew additional guardian angels, larger and more ominous than the previous. Finally he said he was tired. "I'm going to take a nap, Tishrei."

"I'm tired, too, Adar, but you know I can't fall back asleep in the daytime. And the house is so stuffy even with the air-conditioning on. I wish we could open a window. Dad says it doesn't matter, and it's still cool outside. Mom likes to exaggerate everything."

"I have to go to sleep now, Tishrei. I'm really tired." Only then did Adar take off his kerchief.

In the early afternoon the sky on the eastern horizon darkened with thick approaching clouds, as it did before a terrible desert storm.

"Look, Tishrei!" Adar shouted. An insect had landed on the sill of the living room picture window. The creature's hind legs were brown-green and jointed like a frog's, its translucent wings vibrating. Adar ran back to the bedroom to get his magnifying glass.

Suddenly he began screaming. "The window's open!"

Mother came running from her studio. "What's happening! Adar! Adar! Where are you?"

Adar came back into the living room, crying and trembling.

"You left the window open! You left the window open!"

Mother tried to calm him down. "It's all right, Adar. It's all right. I must have overlooked it. I thought I shut the window in your room. I'm sorry. I thought I shut it." She went into the bedroom and came back. "It was hardly open. Now it's closed. Please stop crying."

Adar began whispering to himself, "She left the window open. It was open the whole time. She left the window open in our room."

After Adar calmed down, he held the magnifying glass near the locust that still clung to the windowsill. We all crouched down and took turns watching the exhausted locust move its head slowly back and forth, looking at us with one, then the other black-green polyhedral eye. "Oh, it looks so sad and lonely," Mother said. She smiled nervously. "I guess its friends, our other little guests, will arrive soon enough to keep it company. I wish your father were home for the party."

"It looks sick," Adar said. "It can barely move."

"Maybe he's just resting," Mother said. "He's been traveling a long time. He's come a very long distance."

"It's dying," Adar said. "It's dying."

We heard planes flying overhead. Mother said, "They've just started spraying. See, Adar, we closed the window just in time." The sky overhead was now a starless, moonless night. A light pitter-patter began on the plastic canopies over the garden and on the roof of our house. The noise quickly grew in intensity like hail. All afternoon we heard the planes flying overhead and the locusts raining steadily from the sky. The fallen creatures covered the plastic tabernacles in the yard. They covered our neighbors' houses and they covered the road that led in one direction into town and in the other, over twenty kilometers away, to the research facility where Father worked. Soon the invaders covered all the windows of the house so we could barely look out. Mother got a spatula and went throughout the house banging at all the glass panes to frighten off the locusts, but this did not work. After a few hours the hail noise stopped but there was still the low, sad moaning of the locusts. On the radio we heard that the locusts that had fallen in the Negev would die within twenty-four hours. The vast majority of the invaders, however, moved on overhead in apocalyptic formations, each several miles long, threatening the lush settlements in the north and west. The government said that people and farms in the south had been relatively spared but the threat to the northern settlements was still great. The rabbinate had finally declared a fast, and pre-scribed psalms, prayers, and readings from the Bible.

In the late evening, when Father returned, he skidded on the road in front of the house but then regained control of the car. "It happened three times on my way home," he later told us. "The roads are all slippery with locusts. They're like little capsules of grease."

He entered the screened-in porch. Mother met him there and helped him brush off the locusts that started clinging to him when he got out of the car. "At least they don't bite," he said. "They just tickle." Mother inspected his clothes one final time and with her fingers picked off a few remaining creatures from his shoulder, his zipper, and his cuff. "Okay, you're ready to come out of the decompression chamber. I will turn off the force field." And she led him into the house.

Overnight, while we slept, the great tabernacle protecting the garden collapsed under the sighing weight of the locusts. In the morning my parents went outside to try and salvage what they could, but the task was near impossible. Piles of lo-custs were everywhere, on the collapsed plastic sheets, on the ground, on the house. Under the twisted plastic, most of the plants were severely damaged, their fleshy bodies ruptured, their flowered branches fragmented. Mother began crying un-controllably. "My little babies," she kept saying. "Oh, God, my poor little babies."

Adar watched from the protection of the screen porch. Adar started crying, too. Father began telling Mother that he would plant everything again. "Every single one, Kayla. Every single one." He put out his hand to caress her shoulder but she shrugged him off.

"My little babies! My special babies! I should sit shiva!" With both hands she pulled on the collar of her caftan, rending it.

Suddenly Father's face turned red. His eyes became dark. In a low choking voice that carried over to the porch he rebuked her. "Kayla . . . Even to say such a thing! They're *plants* . . . Have you already forgotten? We sat shiva for a real boy . . . Kayla . . . you will not sit shiva for plants."

I was so shocked that for a moment I could not catch my breath.

Mother headed toward the house, heedlessly trodding over the crunching mounds of insects. She passed through the screen porch. As she entered the house, Adar, still crying, reached up and tried to pat down her torn collar. With an absentminded look, she pushed him away and continued through the living room.

Adar watched as the door of her writing room closed behind her. He stopped crying.

At lunchtime Adar went over to Father, who had stayed home. "My bones hurt. I'm achy."

Father checked his temperature. It was normal. "I don't know what's the matter with you, Adar. Maybe there's been too much excitement." Father went to get Mother, who had not yet come out of her writing room. When she came out she acted as if nothing had happened, as if her special babies had not died, as if she had not been rebuked by Father. As if she had never mourned a real child.

"Well, everything's been topsy-turvy in Galaxy Five. Now let's see what's happening on Earth." She touched Adar's forehead with her lips. "Hmm, I'm not sure." She took his temperature again with a thermometer. It was normal. "Well, you're lucky. I bet the locusts all have a temperature!"

The next morning Adar woke up screaming. "Tishrei, I can't move my right side. I can't move my right side!" His cries woke my parents in their bedroom. A moment later they came running. When they saw Adar they became terrified. Adar was moaning. "Oh, my God," Mother kept saying. "Oh, my God." Father lifted Adar out of bed. His right arm and leg stretched out from his body, they floated out in the bedroom air as if weighing no more than feathers. It seemed as if he might drift out of Father's arms and become a ghost. My parents covered him in a blanket and went out to drive him to the hospital.

Mother and Father stayed overnight in the hospital with Adar. The next morning they all came home. Father carried Adar from the car to the house wrapped in a light blanket.

"I've been poisoned, Tishrei. I almost died, Tishrei," Adar whispered as Father carried him through the living room to the bedroom. My parents stared at each other for a long moment. They were pale and exhausted as if they had not slept in weeks. Mother's eyes began blinking and twitching, something that had never happened before. She stood aside trembling while Father put Adar in bed. She glanced at the floor, at her hands, out a window. She did not speak.

Adar's convalescence was brief. The doctors prescribed a regimen of exercises that Mother and Father did with him several times every day. They stretched out the joints of his arm or his leg, coaxing the paralyzed limb to move.

At the same time Father began the task of replanting and renaming the garden. He ordered plants from nurseries across the country and even took several days off from his research to make sorties into the wilderness. One afternoon, a week after the locusts arrived, Father brought home two strange waist-high specimens. They were almost identical. We had never seen such beautiful plants before.

"I found them near each other in a rock formation. It was hard to dig them out. Look at the shape of their flowers."

Mother watched as Father transplanted the shallow roots into our soil. Father looked up and smiled at Mother. "It looks like they came from Ichalob, Kayla."

She didn't answer.

"It looks like these plants came from Ichalob," Father repeated, still smiling. "They're highly evolved."

"I really wouldn't know anymore." She turned away and went back into the house.

The following day Adar fully recovered the use of his right hand. He sat in his wheelchair in the yard and copied the new succulents in his sketchbook. He drew the graceful weeping branches and the tiny yellow flowers of Elisha's Cure.

The following week Adar was able to walk normally again.

"I'm real lucky I got better from all that nerve poison," he said one night at bedtime. "I could have died or been paralyzed. It's still in my system but I adjusted. You never really get rid of it completely, Tishrei. That's the scary part. You could die at any time."

In the beginning of the summer, Adar received a letter from the National Science Institute. He had, as Father predicted, won first prize in the elementary school category. That afternoon, as a surprise, Mother baked an oval, cell-shaped chocolate cake.

In the evening after dinner she brought it quietly out to the table. On top, in white icing, she had written, "Congratulations, Mr. Mitochondria!"

Adar climbed up and knelt on his chair. He stared at the cake. "Who is Mr. Mitochondria?"

My parents hesitated and looked at each other. A new uncertainty had overtaken them.

"You are," Father finally said.

"Yes, of course, you are, Adar," Mother repeated. "The one and only." And then she added carefully, slowly, as if she had been practicing for a very long time. "Tishrei would have been so proud of you."

"Yes. Tishrei would be very proud of you," Father said.

Adar smiled. "Really? He would?"

"Of course he would."

Adar leaned forward before the great celebration of the cake.

Mother handed him a knife. "Please, Adar, do the honors. It's your cake."

Father said, "Yes. It's your cake, Adar."

"Okay."

Adar stretched out his right hand to cut the first piece. In the strange healing grace of that moment, a faint tremor, a slight vibration moved up his arm.

My parents did not seem to notice this.

I thought I might fall over but I didn't.

I just knelt there, leaning forward, staring at my cake, my right arm outstretched.

From that moment onward, I no longer needed to keep imagining my lost brother.

"Oh, Adar," I heard my parents say to me. They both spoke in the exact same voice, in the exact same breath. My mother and father had suddenly become indistinguishable to me. "Oh, Adar," they said to me, and I realized they were crying. "Oh, Adar, don't you know? We are all so proud of you."

Enfleurage

An egg got caught in one of her tubes. The baby just grew and grew until everything burst.

"Suddenly I saw a great flash and heard, 'Holy, Holy, Holy!' and angels fluttering their wings." Berenice sat forward in a shimmering blue dress and waved her arms in a broad shaft of sunlight. The diamond on her engagement ring glittered.

"It's a miracle I'm alive, only I can never have a natural baby. But I'll never be afraid of Death. I know that Heaven exists."

We were sitting in Berenice's Florida room, leafing through maps and tourist brochures, eating Neapolitan ice cream and madeleines that her husband the cantor had baked. Earlier, at our local Visitors' Bureau, she had moved along the rows of color-ful pamphlets. "One from column A, one from column B . . ."

We were friends at first sight, Berenice said. "Which is a wonderful thing, Alex, with all your mother's going through."

"Thank God the synagogue is finally hiring a cantor," Mother had told me. "It will make life easier for your father. It's hard enough being a rabbi, not to mention writing a book."

Something went wrong with me the summer the Cantor and his wife Berenice moved to Windsor. I was twelve and sometimes, at night, I dreamed I could not swallow. My throat turned to rubber and got stuck. I could not even breathe. I would wake up thinking I was choking and then realize I was all right. I thought I might be going crazy but I never told anyone. Instead, I said my prayers over and over—"On my right is Michoel, on my left Gavriel, before me Uriel, and behind me Refael." I imagined those angels as tall muscular men standing all around me, their fiery swords drawn, their rippling wings outspread, guarding me from danger.

Every week that winter and early spring Mother drove back and forth to Toronto to care for my grandmother. Father was busy writing his book, *The Road to Maḥuza*, about an ancient Babylonian academy in that long-vanished city. "The past moves through us like a graceful ghost," my father would say, "following us up the stairs, climbing in with us beneath the covers, whispering to us, 'Don't forget me, don't forget me!'" After dinner Father would excuse himself. "I'll be in my study writing." Sometimes he would ask if I wanted to help him but usually I said no. With Father one thing led to another. He would say, Please get me this book, which I left on my night table. When I brought that he would say, Please go through that pile of notes and find the page that says Prominent Personalities of

Maḥuza or Agricultural Output on the Fluvius Regum. When I found that he would say, I wonder where I left the new type-writer ribbon, or, I wonder where I put my favorite pen—maybe I left it in the kitchen?

At the end of spring, Mother went to Toronto and brought Grandma back to live with us. Most of the day Grandma stayed quietly in her room, lying in bed or sitting up in a chair, but at night she would wander through the house screaming, "Don't make a liar out of me!" or, "That's a pile of crap! You can't fool me!"

Mother, pale in the hall light, would peek into my room to see if I were awake. "I'm sorry, dear. Grandma's not herself anymore. It's her arteries." I imagined Grandma's arteries dark and twisted and hard like the roots of an old tree. After Mother managed to put her to bed, I would lie awake a long time and remember other things Grandma had said during her rare visits with us. "God, all this religion bores me to death," she once said, getting up from Friday-night dinner, before we sang the Sabbath Hymns or Grace After Meals. And once she told me out of the blue, "Your parents! *My daughter!* What fanatics!"

"Your grandmother is lucky to have such a devoted daughter as your mother." Berenice handed me another madeleine. "Once I read about a woman who kept her old mother in a cage for nine years and only fed her dog food.

"Anyway," Berenice continued, picking up a road map of southern Ontario. "Let's plan some lovely outings."

"These," Father once explained in a sermon, "were created at twilight on the first Sabbath Eve: the Rainbow, Manna, the Staff of Moses, the Shamir Worm that cuts stone.

"They show us that God is the Master Planner, preparing all the events of the world and our lives. Remember, whatever happens, even the smallest thing, is for a reason, never happenstance. Yet we still have free will!"

I believed, too, that God had prepared Berenice for me in that fading light after the birds and fish and trees and grasses of the fields, forming her with his hands from the still-new Earth, breathing life into her with His breath, and sending her to me in the nick of time.

"Call me Berenice," she had said, bending to shake my hand. "'Mrs.' gives me the heebie-jeebies. Like I'm watching myself from a window and don't know who I am. Ever have that feeling?"

The day the Cantor and Berenice moved into a house down our block I had gone over to watch. There were both so tall they seemed giants. "We are smaller creatures than our ancient ancestors," my father once told me. "They were towering in prophecy, soaring with righteousness!" Berenice wore a bright pink dress with matching high-heeled shoes, which made her seem even taller. Her hair was black and wonderfully curled. She smelled like flowers. She carried a birdcage that held a green-and-yellow parakeet. "This is Puccini the Second." The Cantor was watching as the moving men brought in their furniture and boxes. He looked like some old movie star I had seen on television, only heavier, his hair rising like a white wave from his forehead. He turned and smiled at me. His voice was deep and foreign, "Ah, so this is our little neighbor."

That evening they came over for dinner. "I thought you'd be too tired to cook, what with moving and all," Mother said to Berenice.

"I haven't cooked in years. The Cantor does all the cooking and he's wonderful. He lived in France and even invented a dish named after me. Tournedos Berenice. It takes all day to prepare."

The Cantor smiled and smoothed the napkin on his lap with the back of his hand.

Though Berenice only picked at her food, she marveled at each course: stuffed cabbage, roast chicken and potatoes, fruit cocktail. "Delicious! If I eat any more I'll burst!"

The Cantor kept saying, "*C'est bon, Madame,*" or "*C'est un succès fou.*" He told us how he had studied music in Warsaw and later in Paris.

"He dreamed of being a tenor," Berenice said, "and could have been a great opera star, but then came the war. He decided to be a cantor like his father, who was very famous. His father even sang before the Queen!"

I saw myself entering a great palace with Berenice. "Berenice! Berenice!" The Queen rose and held out her scepter as we approached the throne. "Come sit with me. You should be queen, not I. Who is your charming friend?"

After dinner the Cantor sang his own composition, "By the Rivers of Babylon," "in honor of the Rabbi's book." Berenice accompanied him at the piano; her long slender fingers drew a soft melody from the keys. When he got to "We hung our harps upon the willows," my parents cried. I squeezed my fists as tight as possible so I wouldn't cry in front of company.

"There's a touch of *Tosca* in this melody," Berenice said, smiling, and she finished with an arpeggio.

Later Father asked Mother, "She's much younger than he, isn't she? Maybe twenty years?"

"I suppose, but she's a lovely woman."

For some reason these words, "a lovely woman," caught in my head, mixing with the melody I had just heard. They floated round and round in my brain. A lovely woman. A lovely woman. I was filled with these words, though I did not know why. Afterward, whenever I was with Berenice, I would find myself watching her and thinking, A lovely woman, a lovely woman: her hair always done up in thick black curls, her brightly colored clothes, the toe of a high-heeled shoe pressing delicately on the accelerator when we rode in her red convertible.

"It's almost like an island if you think about it." Berenice pointed to Windsor on a map. An orange fingernail traced the blue river above the city, down past Amherstberg, and underneath the peninsula to Lake Erie. I suddenly noticed how the land we lived on dipped like a woman's foot into the water.

"Not only is it like an island, but now, in the summer, it's almost tropical." Berenice started folding the map. "I'd have loved my child to grow up here. Where we are is who we are. Wherever you live, the molecules get into your bones, so when you say I come from Windsor or Toronto or this place or that, it's true, you really do *come* from it. That's why whenever I move or go somewhere new, I like to explore the geography, especially with my best friend." Berenice looked straight into my eyes. "I'm all the places I've been. Winnipeg, where I grew up, and all the places where I've lived since we married, Vancouver and Edmonton and Sainte-Agathe and Pensacola and Scranton, and now Windsor."

"These are some of the things we know from the Talmud," Father explained at dinner. "The people of Maḥuza were rich and lived on a caravan route. They were merchants and farmers. There was always plenty of food and the people drank too much wine. The women were lazy and wore many ornaments and jewels." Father tapped his spoon on the tablecloth.

"But what fascinates me most is that in Babylonia, one academy would rise up and become dominant and eventually decline. Then another would rise to take its place, hence all the famous schools over the centuries: Maḥuza, Pumbedita, Sura, Nehardea."

"I guess you have plenty of material for other books, dear," Mother said.

"I'll probably never get around to them all. Maybe Alexander will take over one day. That's one of the nice things about having a son."

Suddenly, sitting at the table, I could smell my father's study, its yellowing leaves of notes and papers and maps scattered about, absorbing all the oxygen from the room, giving off a sad and musty gas.

"I'm finished eating," I said, and nearly knocked over my chair in the rush to leave the table.

"We're made mostly of water, you and I and everyone," Berenice said. "I think the angels and our souls must also be made of water but in a different state than we know. Not liquid or solid, maybe vapor or something."

She and I had just embarked on the Boblo Boat for the amusement park island. We stood at the railing and looked out at the dark green surface of the Detroit River. Patches of fog from the night before hovered on the surface. "Maybe those are angels," I said.

"Those are angels being born."

"Isn't this crazy and fun?" Berenice's long legs were cramped and squeezed next to mine. She smelled of roses. Our little gondola jerked from side to side as we floated through the Tunnel of Love. Scattered in its dark firmament, little hearts twinkled like stars. Famous lovers glowed and kissed on the walls. She pointed to a smiling crescent moon where a rocking Cupid sat taking aim.

"When I was a little girl I thought the moon was sent to watch over me and everything would work out for the best. You have to believe in something you can see or hear or touch or else how could you go on breathing? I still believe in the moon. Even after what happened to my baby. If my baby had lived, he would be as old as you are and I bet as handsome. My instinct tells me he was a boy."

"Everything happens for a reason, I guess," I said as we floated out into the sunlight.

"Did you have a good time with Berenice?" Mother was boiling a needle and syringe for Grandma's insulin shot when I came into the kitchen. "Let's see. Another ten minutes," she said looking in a little enamel pot on the stove. I told her about the Boblo Boat and how a mist floated on the surface of the water. I didn't say anything about the moon or angels or the Tunnel of Love. I felt too tired to talk about everything, and she didn't seem to be listening anyhow.

"Oh, that sounds nice. I'm glad you have a nice new friend."

That night I dreamed again that I could not swallow. I woke up thinking I was choking. I put my hand on my throat and felt its fine apparatus glide smoothly up and down. I was all right. I fell back into a deep sleep and saw a beautiful guardian angel. Suddenly I realized he was Berenice's son, who was tall and smart and liked me. Now I have the friend I really need, I kept thinking in my dream, now I have a friend. When I woke I felt lonely, because he was gone and I could not remember how he looked.

Everybody loved the Cantor. More people started attending services. Father said, "Soon it will be standing room only." On

Sabbath mornings the Cantor sang many of his own composi-
tions. My favorite was the Aramaic poem "Help Shall Come."

"It's as if the Seraphim were singing!" my father said. "After all, music is the language of the angels. When he sings 'And
When the Ark Traveled,' I close my eyes and float through the
ether of Time!"

Mother even arranged for someone to watch Grandma on
Saturday mornings so she could go to synagogue and hear the
Cantor. I could see her holding back tears as his voice rose to
a high note in "Happy Are Those Who Dwell in Your House."

"Grandma would enjoy his singing," Mother said. This
seemed unlikely to me, since she had never gone to synagogue
when she was well, but my mother was always trying to cover
up for her. "Grandma has had a hard life, lots of disappoint-
ments, that's why she talks like that," Mother would say to me.
"Grandpa, you know, died very young, and she was all alone
with a baby. Deep down she loves all of us more than anything
in the world."

Berenice would arrive just before my father's sermon. For
synagogue she wore dark, rich colors, royal blues or deep reds,
along with white gloves and splendid hats with feathers or silk
flowers or fruit. She would enter the back of the ladies' section
and, sitting down, carefully fold her long legs under the pew
like some glorious bird. Sometimes after services, in the social
hall, she would tell my father she enjoyed his sermon and always learned something new. "I never knew our mother Sarah
had no womb before God remembered her."

Father replied, "Isaac's birth is a greater miracle when seen
in that light."

Enfleurage

I woke up in the middle of the night. Grandma was screaming. "Get away from me! Get away from me! Don't touch me!"

"Ma, I'm not hurting you. I'm helping. Look, your bed is a mess."

"Don't touch me! Don't touch me!"

Later my mother came into my room. "Everything's okay now. Grandma was just upset. She had an accident in bed. It's all that ice cream. That's all she'll eat. I'll have to think of something."

"Look. Can you believe this?" We were driving along the marshlands at Point Pelee. Spread out along the shore were endless miles of cattails and reeds with narrow, zigzagging boardwalks and wooden observation towers for the tourists. Berenice handed me a photograph from her purse. I thought it was a picture of a skeleton. When I looked closer at the knotlike face I realized it was the Cantor. "That's what he looked like when he got out of the camp. You can see what a handsome man he was, even in that condition. Like Maurice Chevalier. I'm sure I would have fallen in love with him even then, though he was so skinny, and I generally don't go for skinny men. As a matter of fact, a doctor, a heart specialist in Winnipeg, wanted to take me out on a date, but I turned him down because he was thin as a stick."

The car slowed and came to a stop on the side of the road.

"You know," Berenice said in such a low whisper I could barely hear, "the Cantor was married once before and even had a baby, a boy, but they were killed. Can you imagine? They rounded them up in the synagogue. Sometimes when he gets quiet, he gets this funny look. His lips move. I think he talks to them in his head. I have to tiptoe around like a ghost. And the Cantor was almost shot. Isn't it amazing, something as small as a bullet can take away a life? Well, my baby was no bigger than a walnut when it almost killed me.

"Now if someone were to ask me if I'm jealous that he was married before, I say, No, no, no, no. The Cantor always says a person can love more than once, and it's true. If not, why would he have married me?

"Puccini the First was a member of the family. She had a tumor on her breast, and I took her to the vet and had it removed. She lived for four years after that. When she died I sat shiva, but only for a day, not a whole week. I loved Puccini the First very much, which doesn't mean I don't love Puccini the Second. I'll be just as upset if Puccini the Second dies."

Mother spent hours in the kitchen making different kinds of food, hoping Grandma would eat something more nutritious than ice cream. "Ma, try this," she would say, giving her a plate of freshly chopped liver or a chicken leg cooked in allspice or even a poached egg with paprika—food my grandmother used to like. "You can't just eat ice cream. Remember your diabetes."

Grandma, her little body shaking with fury, would shout, "Get out of here! Get out of here!" and Mother, trembling, nearly in tears, would leave her room with the rejected plate.

During one of these episodes Berenice came over to pick me up for an outing. We were going to drive to Fort Malden to see the tepees. Mother answered the door on the way from Grandma's room. The plate still trembled in her hands. Berenice entered wearing a beaded Indian dress. Mother was hidden from her, behind the front door. "How's my boy?" Berenice said, seeing me in the hallway. "I'm wearing my Pocahontas outfit!"

"Well, I hope you're not getting spoiled with all this attention," Mother said to me with a funny look on her face.

Berenice saw my mother and smiled. "Oh, no. He's an angel. He's spoiling me!"

Mother merely glanced at Berenice and then went into the kitchen.

"It's true," Berenice said to me in the car. Cornfields stretched out to the horizon on either side of the road. "It's true, you're spoiling me."

"You're my best friend," I said, though it seemed to me someone else was talking, it sounded so silly.

"And you're mine. I'll remember these days forever."

That night I dreamed Mother was cooking something special for my grandmother. She brought the meal to her room on a television tray. The dish was black and smoking. "This I'll eat," Grandma said. "Yes, yes, this I'll eat." Suddenly I realized it was a baby. When she started to eat I was back in my old nightmare. My throat got stuck and I woke up choking.

My father wanted me to read the preface to his book. "All beginnings are difficult," he said, handing me the manuscript. "You should see what my ideas are, since you're my son. Giving birth to an idea is like having a baby! It takes a long time and it hurts."

"That great Leviathan, Time!" Father wrote in the preface. "A living breathing thing. We all live inside and are part of it. Anything that ever happens to Man becomes part of its cells and tissues and organs. And if Time is the creature, History is its soul." While I was reading I glanced up at my father. He was watching me with an astonished look, his mouth slightly open, as if he never knew I could read.

I started having a new nightmare. When I closed my eyes to sleep, I saw Father swallowed up whole by a great ugly fish, like Jonah, rolling inside the dark, slimy guts with no air to breathe. I could see my father deep in the fish, naked, his dark eyes bugging out from lack of light, his screaming mouth open in a great red O. I could not get that picture out of my mind. It invaded my sleep just when I thought my dreams were getting better—since Berenice had come along. Now I knew I must be going crazy. Perhaps my arteries were hardening and soon I'd be like Grandma, wandering through the house at night, screaming, choking on ice cream. I said my bedtime prayers over and over, but that didn't help. I tried to think of Berenice and remember everything she ever said to me, starting from the moment I met her. "The universe is spun from words," Father said. I tried to remember everything Berenice had ever said and done when we were together, so I could watch it like a movie in my mind and fall asleep.

"Smell this. The top note is jasmine. The base is rose." Berenice opened a test tube and dabbed my forearm with the cork.

The scent reminded me of my father. "Jerusalem at twilight," he always said, "has the fragrance of Eden."

Berenice and I were in the Cantor's laboratory, a small room in the basement. "The perfume business is very mysterious," Berenice whispered. "That's why the Cantor never lets anyone in here but me. And sometimes not even me! He must have forgotten to lock the door." In one corner stood an antique cabinet with small glass bottles of various shapes, some transparent, others opalescent, pink and blue and green. I looked up and saw, on top of the cabinet, a silver-framed photograph of a young woman with a baby. "Oh, that's them," Berenice said softly, her long slender arm reaching up for the picture. She handed it to me. The faces were faded and yellow. "Wasn't she beautiful? She must have been nice, too. I better put it back. Here, look at this." On a table in the middle of the room stood a rack of test tubes and a row of flasks. "That's where the Cantor mixes the essences." My foot knocked against something under the table, a large glass jar of blood red roses submerged in an oily liquid. "No harm done," Berenice said. "That's for enfleurage. The oil absorbs the fragrance.

"The Cantor studied perfumery in Paris and has taken it up again. He's a very sophisticated man, just like you're going to be. Perfumery is the most delicate art in the world. He mixed this for me yesterday. The essence bottles just arrived from France. If the Cantor ever invents a new perfume, we could become millionaires. He won't have to sing in a synagogue anymore. Can you imagine if you wanted to be one thing and you had to be something else? How sad that would be. The Cantor should have been an opera singer. That's where his heart is. Sometimes doing the next best thing, like being a cantor, is worse because you're always reminded of what you really wanted to do."

Suddenly the Cantor entered the room. He looked upset. "Now, now, Berenice, you are naughty." He then turned to me and smiled. We all left the room and the Cantor locked the door.

At the end of summer Grandma fell down and broke her hip. She was brought to Hôtel Dieu, where she had a stroke and went into a coma. "A chain reaction," Dr. Lear said to my mother, who now spent all her time at the hospital.

"It's terrible. Old bones snap like sticks," Berenice told me. She told Mother I could stay over at her house if that would make things easier.

"Thank you, but he should stay with his father and help around the house." And later Mother said to me, "Now that Grandma's so sick, I think you should stay home and help your father and not be running around so much with Berenice."

"But we're going to Lake Huron tomorrow."

"Well, after that. Please help your father in the house. It's almost Rosh Hashonah."

"I bet there are dinosaurs buried under all the Great Lakes," Berenice said.

We drove north along the St. Clair River to Lake Huron. It was the hottest day of summer but driving in the car made it seem cool. All along the road little docks jutted into the water. Here and there you could see someone swimming near shore or a small boat sailing by. Because it was a longer trip than usual, the Cantor had made us petits fours iced with bass and tenor clefs and musical notes.

"I don't know how your mother manages." Berenice handed me a grace note. "It would drive me crazy. Before my mother died she just said, 'I'm a little tired tonight, Berenice,' and went to sleep and never woke up. Some people just can't let go. They're afraid of death."

A bee buzzed and skittered across the back of the windshield and then disappeared. Berenice sighed.

"The Cantor's been in another world. He's composing a new melody for the High Holidays. He's been working on 'Behold Like Clay' for three weeks now. He likes to be alone and locks himself up all day. Like a total recluse. Once, when he was composing 'How Goodly Are Your Tents,' he locked himself in his studio every day for three months, though he came out each evening to sing to me what he had written and then made supper. Nothing too complicated, simple things like poached fish or chicken. He still insists on making dinner and baking things, but he hardly eats. He's losing too much weight. I'm afraid he'll turn back into a skeleton!"

Berenice looked at me, her eyes now red. The car swerved slightly toward the side of the road. "This time he hasn't been singing anything to me from his new composition. 'When it's done, Berenice, when it's all done,' he says. I think he must be writing a masterpiece. I'm certain that's what it is. That's the mark of a masterpiece—it can only be played whole."

It was Rosh Hashonah. I had never seen the synagogue so full of people. Extra chairs had been set up in the back and along the aisles to accommodate the great crowd. The tall stained-glass windows were already dark from the night out-side. The evening service was about to begin. The Cantor came and stood next to Father on the altar. They wore full-length white robes and tall white headpieces for the High Holidays. "We dress in the white of the dead to remind us of the final Day of Judgment," Father explained. He nodded and the Can-tor sang "Who Brings the Evening Twilight." In the glowing chandelier light of that holy evening, I imagined all the peo-ple as supernatural beings, souls, phantoms, essences, each dis-tilled like fragrance from a flower. I touched my palm with my fingers and pretended not to feel anything because I, too, was an invisible, vaporous soul. Father then went to the pulpit to deliver his sermon. He had been working on it all that week. "It's the best I've ever written," he had told my mother. "I've dedicated it to your mother's recovery."

In his sermon Father spoke of God's cosmic history and the "stream of harmony He provides for us within Chaos." I looked over to the ladies' section. Berenice, in a dark purple dress, sat smiling, listening to Father.

After the sermon the ark was opened for "Behold Like Clay." As the Cantor rose from his seat, I tried to imagine how his new masterpiece might sound, how it would float over the crowd and fill the synagogue, but I was unable to think of a note. The Cantor stood and looked out past the silent congregation, his eyes slowly searching, his tall figure still. Finally he closed his eyes and began to sing. I knew right then, as his voice spread out through the quiet sanctuary, that this was the most beautiful melody I had ever heard, yet the words were in an unfamiliar language. People started whispering to one another, but the Cantor sang on, his voice now soaring, and the congregation again fell silent. I waited, hoping to recognize the next stanza, "Behold Like Thread," but he did not sing those words either. Only years later did I learn that aria from *Tosca*, though I seemed to understand as the Cantor sang of love on one of the holiest days of the year.

"*E lucevan le stelle*
  The stars were shining
  and the earth was fragrant
  she fell into my arms
  O sweet kisses, o passionate caresses. . . .
  How cruel is Death
  Ah, life was never sweeter!
  E non ho amato mai tanto la vita!"

Suddenly the Cantor opened his eyes as if he had awakened from a trance. His face paled. He staggered slightly, then caught himself. He stood breathing heavily for a moment, then hurried from the altar. A great murmur rose from the crowd and hovered in the air. I turned around. Berenice's face was dead white. She stood up and slowly walked out of the synagogue, staring straight ahead. Father, standing on the altar, seemed tiny in the great expanse of the sanctuary. He lifted his hand and finally quieted the congregation. Then, trembling slightly, in a cracking voice, he began singing the old familiar "Behold Like Clay."

"Berenice came to say goodbye in the middle of the night," Mother told me in the morning. "I'm sorry, but you were asleep, and I didn't want to wake you. You hardly ever sleep well."

I did not understand then why Berenice left Windsor that very night, since it was still the holiday. At first I thought I might cry, but I told myself not to. Do not cry, do not cry, I repeated in my mind. After a few days the Cantor also left. My parents went over to his house to say goodbye but I stayed home.

"It's a shame," I later heard Father saying to Mother. "He had such a gift! The synagogue would have let him stay if he wanted."

Mother was putting on her hat to leave for the hospital. "Yes, it is a shame. And now there'll be more for you to do. Still, I feel sorry for them, especially Berenice. She was very lonely. Oh, I'm late. Grandma will be asking for me."

After all this my nightmares never returned. Instead I would fall asleep before my prayers. I welcomed my sleep. I slept soundly but could no longer quite remember my new dreams. I would wake up with a great yearning, missing someone so badly. Sometimes I awoke thinking it was Berenice I had seen, driving with me along an endless road, or the Cantor singing to me from the altar, beneath the chandeliers, or maybe their son, who rose like a mist from the river and was the friend I had always needed.

DIE GROSSE LIEBE

"*The Great Love* was her best movie. I felt so happy watching her, no matter how many times I saw it."

As always in our house, when my mother described the movie in which her favorite actress starred, she spoke the language of her Berlin youth. Not the jumbled clacking of the crowded Scheunenviertel, noisy with the unsteady tongues of immigrants, but the soft, cultivated tones of the beautiful Grunewald, its grand villas overflowing with art and books and music, its gardens, its lawns sweeping down to quiet lakes.

When she pronounced the film's title—*Die Grosse Liebe*—it sounded to me, a boy born and growing up in the vast present tense of Ontario, so unlike the marvelous emotion it was meant to convey. Despite the gentle refinement of my mother's voice, that sublime sentiment—that grand passion—seemed almost grating and unpleasant. The dense language of my home, the elaborate syntax of my parents' distant, and to me, unknown lives, suddenly became vaguely unsettling.

The revelation that my mother even had a *Lieblingsschauspielerin*—a favorite actress—was a complete surprise and came on the evening after my father's funeral. My mother had never spoken of actors or movies before. As far as I knew, neither of my parents ever went to the movies, although I was allowed to do so. And except for one other occasion, the days leading up to my father's funeral were the only times I could remember my mother leaving the vicinity of our house. She had never gone shopping or out for a walk. I cannot recall her ever taking me to school. I never thought to question this behavior. I had simply accepted it as an aspect of her personality. It was never discussed or explained, and I was rather comforted by her generally quiet and steady presence in my childhood world.

I was only twelve at the time of my father's unexpected death and bewildered by my mother's strange disclosure. She had never been very talkative. But she had, on that exceptional night in my life, suddenly opened a hidden door and—I could not know it then—would permanently and just as abruptly close it again.

"I saw *The Great Love* maybe fifty times the year it premiered. That was the year I stayed with the Retters. Herr Retter took me to his theater, the Gloria Palace, whenever I was sad and needed to get away. I learned every song by heart." My mother smiled and caressed one slender hand with the other. "Sometimes I helped with the projector. I was very mechanical." Here my mother paused and frowned. "The Retters had a daughter my age. Ingrid had dark brown eyes and long black hair. She was a big chatterbox and caused a lot of trouble. *I* was the one with blue eyes and blond hair." My mother gently smoothed a lock of this same hair from her forehead, shook her head, and smiled again. "Of course, like most girls we dreamed of being actresses."

When my mother described the movie in which her favorite actress starred, and whose songs she had memorized, we were sitting together on the living room sofa. The last visitor, an old woman neighbor, had just left. My parents had kept mainly to themselves, and there had been few guests at the house after the funeral. Those who did make the visit included several neighbors, the old woman among them, and some business acquaintances who knew my father from his jewelry store. The old woman had silently helped my mother put away the food that had been set up on the dining room sideboard and then clean up the kitchen. Before she left she took my mother's hand: "I'm very sorry, dear. It's a terrible tragedy. But God is the true judge and we must learn to accept His will." My mother looked at her blankly and said, "Thank you."

Years later, when my mother herself was gravely ill, I took a leave from college to take care of her. She would not allow herself to be admitted to a hospital or permit strangers into the house. I asked her about the old woman. I wondered whatever became of her. My mother lifted her head off her pillow and gave me a surprised look. "Oh, no. There was never such a person that day."

"But there was, Mother. She was our neighbor. I even remember what she said—"

"No, you must be mistaken. And now, Joseph, I'm quite tired."

But I know I was not mistaken and the old woman really did exist. Recently, however, now that I am well into my forties, approaching the ages when my parents died, and I think back to this late exchange with my mother, I find myself increasingly alarmed. I can no longer conjure up a single one of the old woman's features. Did she have a long or short nose? What was the color of her eyes? How did she wear her hair? I recall only a sense of her frail, ghostly movements, the vague disruption of the still atmosphere of our house, and her parting words. The details of our house on that day I remember vividly—the carved oak sideboard in the dining room where the food had been set out on silver platters, the speckled green tiles on the kitchen floor over which the old woman passed, and the claret moiré fabric with which the living room sofa was upholstered.

"In *The Great Love* she played a beautiful singer named Hanna. Oma—whom you never met—was named Hanna, too." My mother had rarely referred to my grandparents except to say proudly that they had been *angesehene Leute*—highly educated and cultured people. Her father, she once told me, had composed art songs in the style of Hugo Wolf, and no doubt would have been famous had he not died, as she put it, *so vorzeitig*—so prematurely. "If you had been a girl, I would have certainly named you Hanna."

The night she told me about her favorite actress in her favorite movie, my mother never looked directly at me. Her eyes skimmed the top of my head and watched the pale blue walls of our living room as if she might be seeing the very same movie, projected there by memory's light. My initial unease at her elaborate reminiscence gave way to an odd comfort and excitement in hearing her talk to me at length as she might have with my father, even if she was in her own world. I had never before considered the mystery of my mother's youth and was now fascinated. I listened carefully and quietly.

While I was growing up, my parents' extreme personal reserve never seemed odd; rather, their conversations seemed dignified and appropriate. In their leisure they read books, or listened to records, mostly lieder and opera. We never went away on vacations. Often they spoke about my father's jewelry store. In the background I would hear references to "a wedding ring with six quadrillions" or "the young woman who bought the emerald pheasant brooch." Several nights a week my mother would go over the store receipts. She sat quietly at a small mahogany secretary in the den. A stack of papers would be piled neatly in front of her while she tapped her forehead with the eraser end of a pencil.

Somehow I grew up understanding that one did not ask questions of a personal nature, even to one's parents. I knew that surrounding every human being was a sacred wall of dignity and privacy. My parents never asked questions such as, "What are you thinking, Joseph?" or, "What did you do today?" They never entered my room without knocking. *"Joseph, darf ich eintreten?"* my mother would say if she needed to do any cleaning. As far as I could tell she never entered my room when I was out of the house. And I am still taken aback, unsettled, observing people who talk too much, chatter, ask question after question.

My mother told the story of *The Great Love* in extensive detail. After her death, I would increasingly find myself reviewing in my mind's eye the scene of my mother's greatest confidence. When I tried to review this night in my mind, I would realize to my great dismay that I had forgotten some small detail, some tangential plot line my mother described, and with it, I felt, some irretrievable clue to her life. Sometimes I would experience physical symptoms when my memory failed me. I would break out in a sweat, breathe rapidly, or feel dizzy. And now, years later, the memory of my mother's description is further clouded by my persistent and pathetic attempts to patch up those gaps, to move through the doorway she had so briefly opened that evening.

The plot of *The Great Love* was—with its predictable twists and turns, period clichés, and movieland formulas—fairly simple. And it was of little interest to me at the time.

Paul, a handsome air force pilot on twenty-four hours' leave, attends one of Hanna's sold-out concerts in Berlin. That night, after the concert, during an air raid, fate brings them together in an underground shelter. They fall in love. But love is not easy in wartime. The next day, Paul had to go on a dangerous mission. Three weeks later, when he safely returns on furlough, they plan to marry right away, but an unexpected order comes in from the High Command. Paul must once again leave abruptly. Meanwhile Hanna, disappointed but still hopeful and understanding, goes on with her life and travels to Paris for her next concert.

"In Paris, Hanna stood onstage in the ballroom of a splendid palace, in front of hundreds of soldiers, many of whom were wounded." My mother sighed. "I kept thinking to myself, Did such places like that ballroom still exist in this crazy world? Yes. Yes. Of course they did! They must. It was an absolutely enchanting scene.

"Hanna wore a black velvet gown with a silver leaf embroidered near the top. Like so." My mother traced an arc across her own bust with her hand. "Hanna was so elegant, so charming, so warm. She stood onstage before a small orchestra. Her accompanist, a sweet older man, played the piano. She sang a wonderful song about how life had its ups and downs but in the end everything would turn out wonderful. And how she knew that one day her beloved, her soul mate, would return."

There were tears in my mother's eyes. I had never before seen my mother cry. She had not cried earlier that day at my father's small funeral, nor had she cried when she came into my room the week before, her face very pale and drawn: "I have very bad news, Joseph. Papi was found dead in his store. We now must survive together."

I asked her only one question that night we sat together on the living room sofa.

"Did Father see it?"

My mother seemed startled by my interruption. "Oh, no. Papi was in a different hiding place. We weren't married yet."

My mother dabbed her wet eyes with a handkerchief. The tears had stopped. "Papi was afraid to go outdoors to come to the theater. Someone might see him and catch him. But once when I was able to go to him, I told him about it. At first he was annoyed. He thought it all foolish, vulgar. Not something I should have been interested in. 'They are wicked people!' he said. 'It's only a love story,' I said. Then Papi said he was sorry and listened, just to amuse me."

After my mother's death, on my first visit to Berlin, I watched *The Great Love* over and over, perhaps five times, all afternoon and evening, at a revival theater on the Kurfürstendamm. Each time I had the strange feeling that my mother was telling me the story as I watched it. Finally the manager came over to me and asked if something was the matter. I said I had come all the way from Canada to see this movie. He shook his head and walked away muttering, "*Noch ein verrückter Fan*—another crazy fan!"

After that a new memory emerged of my mother and her favorite actress in *The Great Love*. It was, I knew from the start, a false memory, but so insistent in nature that even now hardly a week goes by without its coming to mind as if it had actually happened.

In this false memory which has occurred to me ever since I first went to Berlin and saw *The Great Love* myself, my mother gets up from the sofa where she sat with me that night after my father's funeral. She stands up and begins to sing in the voice of her favorite actress. It is that woman's voice but darker and deeper, a voice that hovers between the Earth and the heavenly firmament, singing of miracles to be:

"Ich weiss, es wird einmal ein Wunder geschehn . . .
und ich weiss, dass wir uns wiedersehn!"

But in reality, my mother had been sitting the whole time. She never sang any lyrics. And I never in my life heard my mother sing.

Our house stood on a quiet street at the outskirts of town, and though modest in size, it was densely furnished with sofas and chairs, various mahogany and oak side tables, étagères, and lamps. Except for the kitchen, heavy draperies hung on the windows of every room, including the bedrooms. My mother kept the house meticulously clean. Though she never left the vicinity of the house, and had very little interaction with other people, she always dressed very elegantly, even lavishly. She subscribed to several fashion magazines to keep up with the latest styles. She ordered expensive fabrics from a store in Toronto and made her clothes herself. Often when she was working in her sewing room she would call me over. "See, Joseph, this is a very fine silk, touch it. Feel its weight. Chinese silk is better than Indian. Please hold it out for me so I can see it better," or "This cotton comes from Egypt, the land of Nefertiti, the best cotton in the world."

My mother was also particular about her thick blond hair, which she brushed back from her high forehead and kept gently waved at the temples so it framed her oval face.

My father was always appreciative of my mother's efforts. "Ute, you are very beautiful tonight," or "How elegant you are, Ute," he would say when he came home from work.

"*Danke*, Albert."

My father did the household shopping on his way home from work. From time to time he brought my mother cosmetics, stockings, and even shoes.

Only once, before my father died, can I remember my mother leaving our house. One holiday, I believe it was Yom Kippur or Rosh Hashonah, when I was eight or nine, my father insisted we all go to the synagogue in town. I did not understand why, because we had never attended synagogue before and no one ever expressed an interest in doing so. I can still see my mother adjusting a small feathered hat atop her blond hair. The hat had a delicate transparent veil that hung in front of her eyes. Before we left the house, she glanced in the hallway mirror. She seemed pleased with her appearance. We drove into town for services. While we walked up the synagogue steps, my mother moved with an uncharacteristic awkwardness, constantly looking down at her shoes. I thought she was afraid of stumbling. At home my mother walked very erectly, her tall slender figure moving gracefully.

In the synagogue I stood between my parents and listened to the unfamiliar melancholy singing. I felt sad and bored. My mother leaned sideways and tugged discreetly on my father's sleeve. We moved out in single file from the crowded pew while the singing continued. Later, when we returned home, she looked at my father. She was pale and trembling.

"*Bitte, Albert, nie mehr.*"

"*Ja, Ute, nie mehr. Nie.*"

And we never did attend synagogue again.

When I asked her about that episode before she died, she said, "No. I never went into a synagogue, even as a child. We were never observant. Maybe you went with your father. Perhaps your father took you once. He was very nostalgic."

In my boyhood I began a beautiful and, I did not fully realize then, an extremely valuable gemstone collection. I stored my treasures in a velvet-lined leather case that I hid under my bed. This collection was gently but persistently encouraged by my father. Over time he presented me with many precious and semiprecious stones: an oval-cut ruby, a sapphire cabochon, a violet garnet. "For your birthday," he would say, or, "For your report card." My mother would nod and add, "You must always keep the pretty things Papi gives you. You can take them wherever you go."

"They are like having *Lösegeld,*" my father once said.

"What?" I had never heard that word.

My mother looked sternly at my father.

"Oh, nothing," he said. Later I looked the word up. It meant ransom.

Often I would study my collection under the jeweler's loupe he had given me, which I kept on the desk in my bedroom. He had shown me how to scan a stone's surface and, in the case of a transparent stone, its depths. "A small flaw is a big tragedy if you're a jewel," he was fond of saying.

Once in elementary school, I came home and told my parents that my French teacher, Madame Dejarlais, thought I had an extraordinary gift for languages and that this might be useful in choosing a career for myself. She was right—after college I took a position in Toronto as a translator for a Canadian corporation that was expanding its business in Europe. My mother smiled pleasantly. She was sewing a hem on a dress.

My father said, "That is very good news, Joseph. We are happy to hear it."

My mother looked up from her work. "Yes, of course. We are very happy to hear it."

The next day my father gave me a two-carat marquise-cut emerald, the last gift I received from him. My mother said, "You must always keep the things Papi gives you."

After Paul safely fulfilled his mission, the one he was called to by the High Command, the one that postponed his marriage, he was given three weeks' leave. He traveled to Rome to surprise Hanna, who was rehearsing for her latest engagement. They were joyously reunited and decided to marry that very night. Suddenly, as they were making their plans, the phone rang. An officer friend asked him to help by joining a new and dangerous mission. This time it was not an order but a request. Paul instantly agreed to volunteer.

My mother's voice rose angrily as she described Hanna's reaction. "'Must you go *volunteer* and leave me just like that when we are about to marry! Without so much as an order! What about us? What about our marriage? Is that so unimportant? I cannot, I will not endure this any longer!'"

Then my mother's voice softened. She understood Paul's side as well. "Paul tried to reason with her. It was wartime and he had his responsibilities. 'And what is it you cannot endure,' he asked her, 'when so many awful things are happening in the world?'

"But Hanna remained stubborn and so they broke off their engagement. Paul, dutifully, left on his mission. After he was gone, Hanna sat down and cried."

The morning after my father's funeral my mother knocked early on my bedroom door. *"Joseph, darf ich eintreten?"*

My mother was wearing a sky blue satin dress with long sleeves. There were white cuffs at her wrists and white buttons up the front of the dress. I remembered seeing the shimmering fabric when she was working on it in her sewing room, but I had never imagined the finished product. She appeared especially glamorous to me that day, like one of the models in the glossy magazines to which she subscribed.

"I will be back in the evening." She looked at me to see if I understood and then added, "I cannot sell Papi's store. He loved it too much."

I was puzzled, not because of the sudden and astonishing discarding of what clearly was some form of phobia. I never thought in such psychological terms when I was a child. I was puzzled mainly because it was three miles downtown to my father's store and my mother did not drive. I could not picture her, dressed in white-trimmed, sky blue satin, walking that distance, or for that matter, traveling on a bus, though it would have been simple to do so.

"I must go now, Joseph. The taxi is waiting."

For the next two years she went back and forth by taxi from our house to the store. She did not, as far as I knew, go anywhere else. I believe the store must have been for her an extension of our home. I took over from my father and did all the food shopping. My mother would give me a list with the brand names she preferred. Sometimes she asked me to buy certain cosmetics or stockings as my father had done for her. In her spare time she continued to order material from Toronto and make her own clothes.

My mother turned out to be a skilled businesswoman and was good with customers. She still sold jewelry as my father had, but she expanded her merchandise to include fine gifts, such as crystal and silver. Though at home she continued speaking to me in German, her English was much better than I had realized, and her accent diminished over the time she worked in the store. Occasionally I would catch her at home with her sewing, repeating some English word out loud until she was satisfied with her pronunciation. Once she caught me watching her. She smiled. "A good actress must adjust her accent for a new role."

My mother continued my father's custom of building up my gemstone collection. On the first anniversary of his death, she gave me a one-and-three-quarter-carat round-cut diamond. I examined it that night under my loupe. I scrutinized its brilliant surface table, the glittering facets of its crown and pavil-ion. Its depths were flawless and fine white. My mother asked if she could enter my room. She took the loupe and examined the diamond herself.

"Yes, it is really an excellent stone. You must keep it with all the things Papi gave you."

Sometimes after school or on Saturdays I helped my mother at the store. One day, near the second anniversary of my fa-ther's death, a short, dark-haired woman came into the store. No other customers were present. The woman wore expensive clothing, large sunglasses, and many rings on her fingers. She walked around the store, browsing. She looked at me, then my mother. My mother smiled. "May I help you, please?"

The woman answered in German. "Yes. Would you show me those bracelets?"

"Natürlich." My mother leaned over to open the display counter.

The woman took off her sunglasses and glared at the blond hair on my mother's bent-over head. "Feuchtman," she whis-pered. "Feuchtman." It took me a moment to realize the woman was saying my mother's maiden name. My mother had rarely mentioned it. My mother looked up. She smiled. *"Wie, bitte?"* To this day I don't think my mother actually heard or understood that the woman had just called her name. Suddenly the woman whirled around, her scrawny arm outstretched, her fist slamming into my mother's jaw with surprising force. One of my mother's teeth flew out, clattered across the glass top of the display cabinet and then fell to the floor.

My mother stood up. Blood gleamed at the corner of her mouth. She was so startled that she did not even bring up a hand to feel the damage on her face.

"Petzmaul! Verräterin!" The woman spat at my mother. "Bitch! Traitor! You are worse than they were! The evil informer-girl is finally caught!"

The woman ran out of the store and disappeared. I heard a car speeding off but I was too shocked to run out and look for the license plate. I did not even move from where I was standing.

Finally my mother spoke. Her voice was altered because her lower jaw was now swollen. I could barely make out what she said. When she spoke she did not look directly at me. Her eyes skimmed the top of my head as they did the evening after my father's funeral, when she watched the pale blue walls of our living room and told me about her favorite actress in her favorite movie. She whispered.

"Oh, no. No, no. She is completely mistaken. I would never have worked for them even if they tortured me. I would never turn anyone in. How could I? . . . I had to do something to save your father. . . . No. No. I myself was hiding the whole time, first with the Retters . . ." She became silent. She wiped her mouth, then felt her jaw, opening and closing it slowly. She smoothed her blond hair back with both hands. She took in a deep breath and looked directly at me. "Well, no bones are broken. There is no need to see a doctor. You know I do not go to doctors. Why are you shaking?"

A week later she put the store up for sale.

According to city records, the Grunewald house, where my mother grew up, was destroyed during the war. Now, in its place, are pretty garden apartments with cobblestone trails meandering down to a small lake. The house of my mother's favorite movie actress in nearby Dahlem, across the street from a forest park, is now a retirement home.

A few years after my first visit, my company established a permanent office in Berlin. I requested a transfer. I thought of renting one of the garden apartments where my mother's house once stood, but none was available. Instead I found an apartment south of the Tiergarten and have lived here almost as long as my parents lived in Canada. At night, from my small balcony, I can see far across the lights of the Kurfürstendamm into the vast city. In *The Great Love*, Hanna had a balcony, too. In one scene she stands there with Paul looking out at the sparkling night sea of Berlin. "It is like a fairy tale," she says sighing.

"No," Paul answers her. "It is lovelier than a fairy tale."

I don't think it would be an exaggeration to say I have seen *The Great Love* more than fifty times. When I first moved to Berlin I would see it anytime it was playing at the revival houses, which was surprisingly often. Later, when it became available on video, I began watching it at home. I have also seen my mother's favorite actress in her other movies: *To New Shores, In the Open Air, Homeland.* But I found these other movies boring and never went to see any of them a second time.

My wife never asks me questions about this peculiar obsession of mine. She thinks only that I am a crazy fan. There are so many other people here who are fascinated with my mother's favorite actress. She is a great cult figure. If you go to the clubs you are bound to find someone dressed up like her, singing her songs, "Could Love Be a Sin?" or "My Life for Love." My wife is glad I have not come to that. *"Ich bin sehr dankbar dafür!"* she says. I am thankful for other things. Though we have now lived together for many years, she does not ask me about my family, nor do I ask about hers. I like to think of our life together as in the present, so long as the present maintains its own sense of privacy. Even in *The Great Love*, Paul and Hanna do not ask each other questions of a personal nature.

Lately, now that I am approaching the ages of my parents' premature deaths, when I recall my mother on the night of my father's funeral, I see us sitting on the claret moiré sofa as *The Great Love* is projected on the pale blue walls of our living room. We are watching it together. My mother takes my hand and smiles. She is enjoying herself so much and she hopes I am, too.

After Hanna and Paul break up, Paul leaves on his new mission, the dangerous mission for which he has nobly volunteered. Hanna remains in Rome rehearsing for her big concert.

Her concert is, of course, an amazing success. As she walks triumphantly offstage, she is handed a telegram. "Captain Paul Wendland has been wounded but only slightly. He is in an infirmary in the mountains." As Hanna returns to the stage and takes her bow, she whispers to her accompanist that she must leave that very night.

"Hanna, when will you return?" he asks sadly, for he is obviously in love with her, too.

"Nie."

My mother recited this "Never" with the same restrained tone of conviction, the precise note of love and hope that I later witnessed each time I watched her favorite actress in her favorite movie.

Finally Hanna arrives at an infirmary somewhere in the Alps. Snow-covered mountain peaks are all around. She rushes over to Paul, who is sitting on the terrace, one arm in a sling. "Perhaps, Hanna, we can try again to get married." He laughingly points to his bandaged arm. "This time I really have three weeks' sick leave!"

Hanna smiles. She takes his hand. "And after the three weeks are over?"

Paul looks up and she looks up, too. Overhead, the sky is so wide and breathtaking. Here and there, glorious shafts of sunlight break through the billowing clouds. And suddenly, in the distance, a squadron of planes appears. And there, of course, to those wondrous heavens, Paul must return. That is where his duty lies.

"Paul turned and looked into Hanna's eyes," my mother told me. "Their faces were so beautiful, so full of happiness, it gave me goose bumps. And then Hanna nodded. Yes. Yes. She would marry him."

And then my mother turned and looked directly at me for the first time on that extraordinary night in my life. I trembled ever so slightly at the unbearable tenderness of her look. "If I had been them," my mother said, rising from the sofa, "I would gladly have sacrificed all of heaven for love."

THE ADORNMENT OF DAYS

❧   ❧   ❧

Alexander Sahne rises from his desk, slowly, majestically, as the Divine Shekhinah shall surely rise, on the day of Her choosing, from the dust of an earthly Exile, raising the sparks of fallen souls with Her. Alexander's bearing—head held high, black hair flowing—is magisterial, redemptive, though he is of medium height and slight build, and completely naked.

It is an unusually hot Jerusalem morning, the Saturday before the great fast of Tisha B'Av, and outside, on the sloping street below his window, the people walk to their synagogues in a silent torpor.

He crosses to the mirrored wall of his studio, formerly his Opa Jacob's study, in the apartment he has inherited from his mother's father and to which he has fled from the clamor of New York City.

He tapes a sheet of pale green music paper, his dawning sense of the Shekhinah's voice, on the mirrored wall, among a slowly growing matrix of sketches notated in his meticulous hand. He becomes agitated thinking of this voice, this personality, and all the music he has yet to compose, which somehow must reveal God's feminine aspect Who dwells in Creation.

A *bat kol*, a heavenly voice, not unlike the nagging chorus of the crowd, now descends and asks, What is the purpose of this display? Why? Why?

"This papery web," Sahne answers aloud, with a dramatic flourish of his arm, as if onstage, "this fluttering scaffolding gives me a sense of structure and form on which to build my opera, or, perhaps"—and this he adds in a low and confidential whisper, his hand to the side of his mouth—"or perhaps, it doesn't."

But Sahne, speaking in the lonely room, addresses not only the unseeable crowd, the elusive audience, but also his own essential self, the form that stands just outside his peripheral vision, the invisible hand that for so long has led him out of his youth, always ready to protect, to inspire, or advise. How else has he, in his thirty-one years, managed to write, with a furious propulsion and a relentless imagination, with steadily increasing acclaim and anxiety, three piano and two violin concerti, four symphonies, and numerous chamber works? And under what other agency will he be able to complete his first opera?

Sitting down again, he scans the harmonic shape evolving across the mirrored wall, a gradual accretion that seeks to obscure the reflected world of Sahne at his desk.

Once Sahne asked his grandfather, "Opa, why did you cover this wall with mirrors?"

"Sasha, *mein Liebling,* after your mother married and left for so far away, I became always alone in here. Who would know if I'm dead or alive? I wanted to be able to look up and be certain!"

Now, looking up, Alexander is uncertain where in this visual template, in this temporal sequence, he should place the Adrianople bedroom scene, a scene he has just begun to conceive.

What he is sure of is this: in the Adrianople bedroom scene, the messianic pretender, the false redeemer, Shabbatai Ṣevi, a beautiful tenor, in one of his states of illumination—when to look on his face was to look on the countenance of the moon—will force the Shekhinah to appear by invoking Her secret and holy Name. And the Shekhinah, at first angered by this impudence, will be swayed and seduced by his exquisite declaration of love.

Sahne bites habitually around his fingernails. He holds his hands up, inspecting the latest damage. The skin is raw and torn along his left thumbnail.

"My hands are shaped like yours," his mother had once said long ago, as if she had inherited her delicate, well-shaped hands from him instead of the other way around. She came and sat alongside him at the piano bench, interrupting, something she never did. She gently placed his hand in her own. She spoke slowly, shaking her dark wild hair out of her eyes with a toss of her head. "Yes, my hands are like yours, Sasha, but your destiny," and here she pointed to a differentiating line angling across his palm, "is, thank God, expanding, independent, luminous, while mine has been, well, I don't know . . ." She sat there next to him lost in thought.

"Mom, I'm working."

"Working? You're only nine years old." She looked down at her lap. "Well, I suppose that's good. I should be getting back to mine. Translating Opa's latest book is so difficult. I'm beginning to hate Shabbatai Ṣevi! He was such a coward, especially for someone who thought he was the Messiah. When he came to the Sultan to demand the keys to Jerusalem, the Sultan gave him a choice, convert to Islam or die, and he chose to save his own skin! He was sick and pathetic, and Opa spent seven years studying him!" She stood up and leaned on Alexander's shoulder. She forced a smile.

"I'm proud of you, Sasha. You have a great gift. But sometimes I'm afraid you're missing your childhood."

He felt heavy inside. She had never spoken to him like that before. She had always been the one who encouraged him. When he was seven, she had arranged for private theory and composition lessons at the conservatory, and to celebrate, she bought him a rebuilt Steinway baby grand to replace the old spinet he had begun playing at age four.

"If he's going to compose," he overheard her saying to his father in the dining room, "then he needs to *really* hear what he is doing."

"I understand, Chaya, I do, but we just can't afford it right now. Four thousand dollars! And you went out and bought it without even telling me! I'm only a simple yeshiva principal, not a Reichmann. We can't afford it."

"Of course we can. My mother left me some money." Her voice was light, careless.

"But I don't see how—"

"Well, we can!" she said, now angry, and slammed a door behind her.

Later his father said, his face paler than usual, "Sasha, your mother and I know you'll work hard at your music, that's why we want you to have the best piano. Yes, the best. We thank God for the gift He has given you. You know, the Bais Hamikdash reverberated with music and song. Perhaps you will write the music for the rebuilding of the Temple, may it happen speedily in our days."

Sahne gets up again, calmly, and goes over to the window, where he can better inspect his hands in the bright sunlight. He turns and flexes them this way and that, slowly, as the hands of a Balinese dancer might move to the staggered rhythms of the gamelan. But his agitation returns and grows, until he suddenly realizes, bathed in the window light, that the obvious difficulties in representing an invocation of the Shekhinah's ineffable Name should be achieved with a pure and wordless vocalise. And this realization—which to Sahne seems perfect, so eternal and so true that it must have its counterpart in some higher realm—fills him with something near bliss.

He stands before the window, eyes closed, his lids and the pulsing caverns of his mind transilluminated by the sun. And he suddenly hears, in sweeping and glorious bitonal progressions—A major with F-sharp minor, E-flat major, and C minor—the whole host of heaven, singing before him.

Although Opa Jacob dedicated his long academic life (*"mein neues Leben"*—my new life—he referred to his life after fleeing Germany and coming to Palestine) to several heavy, densely written tomes, Sahne has confessed, in an interview in *Opera News*, that he has only recently begun to read, in preparation for his opera, his grandfather's most famous work, his esteemed, essential, all-consuming *A History of Normative Kabbalistic Thought and the Sabbatean Heterodoxy*.

"My mother translated all his writings for the Oxford series. I think in this sense she was an artist, because everything reads so beautifully, though it is all very convoluted. But it didn't help her delicate emotional state. Actually, I think it exhausted her, though she loved my grandfather."

And now Sahne feels, in the increasing heat of the late morning, a warm lingering presence, the old man's *Hochdeutsch*-inflected faith, his relentless astonishment.

"Wach auf, Alex! Es gibt ein Wunder!" his grandfather had called out fifteen years before, when Alexander was sixteen, waking him in this same apartment on another sweltering morning and, shuffling in his house slippers, pulling him from a late, deep, jet-lag-induced sleep to a window. Alexander's mother had just died, and he had come from Manhattan to spend August with his grandfather.

"I don't see anything, Opa."

The tall old man pointed.

In the distance a billowing fog rolled swiftly toward the baking city, dissolving the enclaves on the northern and western hills, swallowing the Knesset and its grounds, finally enveloping his grandfather's quiet and pious neighborhood. The transformed atmosphere was now cool and refreshing.

"Aus Paradies!" his grandfather said in a wide-eyed, incredulous tone, waving a thin white arm out the window through the dense cold mist. "I have never witnessed such a natural phenomenon! Salvation from the wilderness!"

His grandfather turned away from the window, withdrawing his arm from the fog. He smiled expectantly.

Alexander knew his grandfather wanted to hear some words indicating Alexander's own susceptibility to joyous astonishment, and so prove that this facility, this true and essential faith, could skip a generation—Alexander's melancholy parents—and appear again, a dominant trait in a newer life. But just then Alexander became distracted and could say nothing. He heard clearly a fragment of melody, a mood. He abruptly excused himself to write it down, afraid the notes might evaporate in the volatile air.

He worked steadfastly, furiously. In three days he developed the melody into sonata form, scoring it for piano and violin. On the Friday morning it was finished, he went into his grandfather's study.

"Opa, where is your violin? Would you play with me?"

Alexander sat at the piano in the living room, while his grandfather went to the bedroom closet and took out his old violin. Opa Jacob took a long time to tune. "*Ach,* it is an old and sickly friend. When I first came here we used to have musical evenings, me, Oma, may she rest in peace, at the piano, and some colleagues from the university."

The first notes came tentatively, his grandfather narrowing his eyes and leaning forward to read off the music stand. "I am out of practice and my eyes are bad. I hope I can do your piece justice." But soon they were moving through the music with confidence, Opa Jacob gently swaying. Suddenly, the old man's bow trembled, he stopped playing, his eyes overflowed. *"Es ist so schön, Alexander. Du bist wirklich ein Wunderkind!"* And then Alexander thought he heard an escaping breath, a sad soft obbligato, the name of his mother, his grandfather's only child: "Lotte."

His grandfather shook his head. "We must continue! *Weiter! Weiter!"* They played it through several times until his grandfather said, "Ah, I am so hungry! I'll make us something good for lunch, Sasha, to celebrate. This work is so passionate. Too passionate for a sixteen-year-old boy! And passion, you know, Sasha, makes one hungry."

Opa Jacob shuffled again in his house slippers into the kitchen, moving from the refrigerator to the stove and back, rambling through the territory of his youth.

"When I was a boy, Sasha, I studied piano and violin. Children in all good homes did. Once, when I was your age, I went to the Berlin premiere of Korngold's opera *Die Tote Stadt.* My father knew his father, they were distant cousins. You will laugh at me, Alexander, an ancient figure who stands on the precipice, but I thought to myself, I would give anything if I could only write such sublime music! It was only a thought, of course, because I had no talent. But it was a deep, insistent, transcendent thought." He looked proudly at his grandson, placing in front of him a plain, runny omelet garnished with tomatoes and cucumbers. "Perhaps you have inherited the thought from me. There once was a kabbalist in Gerona who believed that thoughts, profound thoughts, could be inherited!"

Opa Jacob sat down across from Alexander and opened a small yogurt for himself. He sighed.

"The music was sublime," he began again, distracted, spooning out of the small white container. A thin white mustache formed on his upper lip. Alexander, momentarily disappointed, realized his grandfather was still referring to the Korngold opera, not his own new sonata. "Oh, it seemed a great success. Well, that poor genius has been unfairly overlooked. That is a frightening thing to consider. Do they teach you about him at your conservatory?"

Alexander said he had heard his name but did not know his music.

"Ah, you must try to learn it!"

He then began singing in a clear falsetto, startling Alexander,

"*Gehe hinaus ins Leben*
  Go out into life,
  Another calls you—
  See, see and understand."

His grandfather explained. "The ghost of a young and beautiful woman steps out of her portrait and sings these words to her mourning husband. I still have an old recording of the aria by Lotte Lehmann, a funny thing to carry along when one is trying to escape. The story is actually quite silly, like all German opera, but *ach*, the music!

"But even such music could not save us from those terrible

days. People always worry about these questions, then write books about them, 'Art and Evil,' 'Music and Cruelty.' But music, after all, is only an adornment of time."

"Opa, perhaps you could have been a composer, or at least a soprano!"

His grandfather laughed. "*Nein*, Sasha, and I am not complaining. You, of course, are different. I was fortunate to have other interests as well. But music is one of the reasons I was drawn to Ṣevi. Ṣevi's admirers and critics alike, in the documents I found during my research, all agreed that the sweetness of his singing was one of his strongest attractions."

He looked at his grandson.

"You know, Opa, Mother always hated Ṣevi because he was such a great coward. She said that when the Sultan gave him an ultimatum, he should have chosen death and martyrdom. Why didn't he, Opa? What do you think?"

His grandfather reached across the table and grabbed Alexander's wrist. His grip was unexpectedly tight. "*Sag mir. Warum hat sie das getan?* Why? Why?"

But Alexander could not answer for his mother, for the mystery of a scholarly woman, the daughter of a scholar, who, alone one afternoon, peered into a kitchen oven as if searching for something, and turned on the gas.

Now, fifteen years later, sitting in the Jerusalem apartment, Alexander closes his eyes and holds his breath. He begins to hear the melody of his sonata again, his own piano playing and his grandfather's tremulous bow work. He passes a hand through his hair, which is so thick and black that his mother once said, in the year before her death, "It is one of your many luxuries, Alexander. I've always wondered why hair, which is the dead part of our bodies, is so tied in with desire and strength. Like in the story of Samson and Delilah. Well, sometimes, Alexander, I don't have any answers." She paused and stared at him. She had just been released from one of her increasingly frequent stays in the hospital. His father had warned him, "Mother cannot help it, she's still not herself yet, but it's good she is coming home. This is where she belongs." Alexander looked at his mother and felt a great uneasiness. "Mom, can I play you something? You always liked 'O Wüsst' Ich Doch den Weg Zurück.'"

She did not seem to hear him and continued, "Sometimes, Sasha, a desire, even the strongest one, simply dies and there is nothing you can do about it."

And now he yearns, in the intense memory of the melody and the disquiet of those words, for a strong warm hand to trace the shape of his head, the breadth of his shoulder, and the curvature of his back. Somehow he had lost that early sonata manuscript. He had performed it only once, shortly after his visit to his grandfather, at one of his conservatory recitals. He had called it, though he knew even then it was unfortunately named, "Charlotte's Lied." For it was clear then as it is now that the piano line is nothing if not a tenor voice, and this thought had endured as such all these years in some deep network of his brain. It hovers now, enticing him in the morning heat, masculine, sweet, seductive. He sketches in three staves, the melody and accompaniment. He immediately understands, and this, too, is a moment of relief and joy, that this musical beckoning, this melancholy-sweet bridge across the years, is the leitmotiv of the false messiah, the seducer of the lonely Shekhinah and the souls of the Jewish people, the tenor voice of Shabbatai Ṣevi.

In the late morning, Alexander envisions the opening scene of his opera. Above, suspended in the air, is a cloud-disguised platform carrying the heavy Chorus of the Dead. Below, at stage level, is a poor congregation gathered in their synagogue. A *maggid*, a traveling preacher, stands at the pulpit and foretells the imminent arrival of Shabbatai Ṣevi, the King Messiah, and all the wonders of the newly dawning age. When the Chorus of the Dead overhear the prediction of their resurrection, they become delirious with joy and begin to sing and dance. All in all, it would be a complex and expensive production, and Sahne is glad he does not have to concern himself about cost. He writes a note to Gloria X.

"*The Adornment of Days*, which is what I've finally chosen to call my opera, is taking its form, and form must always precede music. It emanates in tiny increments on the walls of my grandfather's studio, in the mystical way the Shekhinah emanates from the Infinite One to live in and sustain Creation."

Gloria X had first heard his music performed, his suite for strings, entitled *The Mystery of the Godhead*, on a Channel 13 television broadcast. She telephoned him the next day and introduced herself. She spoke *sotto voce.* "Unfortunately, Maestro

Sahne, one of the nerves to my voice box is paralyzed from an otherwise successful operation. Can you hear me all right?

"I hope I'm not being presumptuous in saying so, but I would guess from *The Mystery of the Godhead* that your music is meant for the voice, and the voice is meant for your music! I can help you. Come see me, Mr. Sahne—that is, if your schedule permits."

The next day he met with Gloria X in her rambling Sherry-Netherland suite. Tall, slender, fiftyish, she answered the heavy oak door herself, wearing a black silk sari. Voluminous gray-blond hair fell softly on her shoulders. A small brooch of pearls and sapphires was clasped to her neckline. She took him by the hand and said in her raspy, whispery voice, "I'm so glad you could come see me, Maestro Sahne. This way, please."

He saw no servants. Several longhaired white cats slunk in and out of the rooms. Sahne could not help staring at their exotic faces, round and flat, not at all catlike, with large eyes.

"Their hearts are so fragile," Gloria X said sadly, "that they often die young. That is the main drawback of their breed. Come, Maestro Sahne, one must avoid falling in love with them."

She led him by the arm into a large airy room with floor-to-ceiling windows overlooking Central Park. They sat down facing each other in two magnificent chairs, each with enormous, outstretched carved wooden wings. "Wendell Castle designed them for me, you know," she said, smiling. "They are my angel chairs." And sitting there, before the open view, she appeared to be hovering above the green earth in the arms of a giant seraph.

"When you took your bow, Maestro Sahne, I was surprised

to see such a young and handsome man, what with all your accomplishments and awards. Well, I said I can help you. Am I right in assuming you might want, or perhaps need, to write an opera?"

He was astonished by her impending offer. He tried to remain calm.

"May I ask why you want to commission an opera?"

"As a memorial." She leaned down to stroke the fur of a cat brushing up against her leg. "My only child died two years ago. She studied voice. But I won't talk about her because I do not want to influence the topic you may decide upon. I am not expecting an opera *about* my daughter. You are completely free. I suppose, too, that you already have some ideas."

"I do. But I'm afraid my idea would need a great deal of support. Operas take so long to write and then, well, production costs—"

"Maestro Sahne, I make things happen. Tell me."

So he began telling her about the seventeenth-century messianic pretender Shabbatai Ṣevi.

While Sahne was speaking, she fluttered two fingers in the air. A maid entered the room with a tea tray, placed it on a high narrow table between them, and left.

"Please, continue, Maestro." Gloria X poured him a cup of tea.

Sahne went on to describe the kabbalistic underpinning of Ṣevi's messianic movement, which had electrified world Jewry, leading individuals to sell their homes and property in preparation for their imminent departure to the Holy Land. And finally the mass theological confusion caused by Ṣevi's shocking conversion to Islam. "The Sabbatean sects that developed in the aftermath were full of paradoxical beliefs and rituals. They confused sin with virtue. My concept of this opera is, after all, embryonic, not much more than an idea, though I do have one revolutionary—"

Sahne accidentally dropped his teacup, which shattered on the mahogany floor, splattering its contents. He turned pale and felt dizzy. The saucer drooped in his hand.

Gloria X remained perfectly still, staring at him. She again fluttered two fingers in the air. The maid came quietly into the room and quickly swept up the china pieces into a small dustpan. She mopped up the liquid with a white linen towel.

Sahne leaned his head back in his chair. "I'm really sorry about that."

Gloria X didn't move. She didn't even seem to be breathing.

Sahne continued nervously. "I want the Shekhinah to be a character in the opera, the love interest of the self-deluded Şevi, though I don't know yet what She will do or say. *The Mystery of the Godhead* that you heard, if one can relate music to anything in the real world, related in part to the Shekhinah's place in the mystical hierarchy of the Infinite God. It did not address Her personality or Her voice. But I think it is a good starting point for the ideas I would like to develop in my opera."

Gloria X's glazed eyes now fixed on a point high above his head. Sahne nibbled at his fingernails, worried he was talking too much and sounding crazy.

Gloria X slowly brought her pale hand to rest gently above her breast. She drew in a breath. "Astonishing!" She began to rise from her angel chair but sat back down again. "How astonishing. A false messiah *and* a woman God."

Sahne was relieved. After another pause she continued, "Astonishing! An opera with meaning and history."

"But I don't want it to be a history lesson. I want the story, the heavy scholarship that now surrounds and suffocates it, to be *verklärt*—transfigured."

"Ah, yes, of course. You are so right."

"Yes, but what I mean, what bothers me, is the prosaic historical ending. Ṣevi comes to the Sultan to demand the keys for Jerusalem, and the Sultan says convert or you're dead. And Ṣevi simply acquiesces and becomes an apostate, betraying the hopes and beliefs of thousands of followers. He's a coward. It's annoying. He didn't have the decency to become a martyr, though I can't say I blame him. But I don't know how to get around that. How to make Ṣevi's choice important, significant. Not just a craven act, which is boring. Anyway, I hope that you, I mean, people nowadays, won't find this topic too obscure or ethnic."

Gloria X smiled. "Why, Maestro Sahne, my family has only recently become goyim. Three or four generations at most! The Parisian root of my now thoroughly Christian—and now unfortunately, in some cases, dreadfully evangelical—family has long prided itself in being descended in part from intelligent and learned Jews. But historical upheavals strengthen the life force for all of us, and everyone benefits, don't they? And who would write the libretto?"

"I must write it myself."

"Ah, a modern Wagner!" Gloria X clapped her hands together once, which made no more noise than if they had been feathers.

"Well, it may take a little time to arrange things. And I hope you will understand, Maestro Sahne"—she said this with the most charming smile—"ever since my daughter died I am no longer accustomed to seeing people very often, even people I so admire. It is a great effort for me. But I think with you it will be different. Anyway, be assured, you will not be abandoned."

And so, by the following week, Gloria X called to tell him she had obtained a commitment from the Lyric State Opera. "Karl Heinz, the director, was once, briefly, in the days when I bothered with such things, my husband, and my daughter's father."

Sahne then received a letter of intent in which her foundation guaranteed him a handsome grant as both composer and librettist, freeing him from his teaching and allowing him to move for an indefinite time to the apartment in Jerusalem. And Gloria X added in a postscript, "Please, don't worry about production costs. They are a trifle."

In the early afternoon Sahne stops working. Though the stores are all closed for the Sabbath, he thinks he might walk downtown and window-shop for an air-conditioner. He makes his way along the cypress-lined Ramban Street. The walk toward the center of the city, the still heat, fills him with longing.

He turns down Agron Street and enters Independence Park. He wanders along the dirt trails among the flowers and dusty shrubbery. The glances of the strolling men, their dark limbs, intoxicate him. He walks to the eastern part of the park, an area of old faded gravestones inscribed in Arabic.

Tired, he sits down on the edge of a dry, ancient reservoir, the Mamillah Pool, at the far end of the gardens. He closes his eyes. He is startled when he feels something, a fine foot in a black loafer, grazing his thigh. Alexander looks up and sees a handsome young face.

"I remember all my dreams and I know I've dreamed of you."

"I'm glad for that," Sahne says. He wishes he had brought along something to drink, he is so thirsty. He feels a headache coming on, but the young man is so beautiful. Sahne has never seen such green eyes.

The young man begins climbing down the steep wall of the cistern. "I will tell you something."

Sahne follows him cautiously. The young man is graceful, slender, agile, like a mountain animal. He stretches out his hand to help Sahne. His hold is firm, searching, the skin of his palm smooth and dry. Sahne thinks he must be in his early twenties. A small cloud of dust rises when they land on the floor of the cistern.

"Sometimes I dream I'm an eagle, sometimes a leopard. I know I have dreamed of you. My dreams always teach me what to do. Where are you from?"

Sahne tells him he is from America, but staying in Jerusalem. "My family is from here."

"Mine, too."

The young man does not ask any more questions but Sahne tells him, "I'm writing an opera." Sahne blushes. It seems a silly thing to say standing at the bottom of an ancient reservoir among broken bottles, sturdy weeds, and crushed, faded cigarette boxes.

They go off into a corner behind a pile of boulders. Later the young man offers him a cigarette but Sahne doesn't smoke.

"In this life I am a poet," the young man says. "I remember all my dreams. Last night I dreamed I was an eagle. And now I know why I was flying so much. I was looking for you."

"Who are you?"

The young man smiles. "Sami. But I have to go now."

Sahne watches as Sami hurriedly climbs up the reservoir's wall and disappears over the edge. An invisible voice calls down to Sahne in the depths.

"I am an eagle and I will find you again."

When Sahne arrives at the apartment the answering machine in the hallway is blinking. He ignores it and goes into the kitchen. He is dusty and had almost fallen and killed himself while climbing out of the reservoir. He drinks a liter of cold water from a pitcher in the refrigerator. He imagines the miraculous substance diffusing throughout his body, entering his tissues and his cells. He needs a shower.

His grandfather had used a small plastic chair, which Sahne takes from the corner of the bathroom and places in the shower stall. He sits down and lets the cool water flow over him. He feels he is still dehydrated and walks back, naked and dripping, to the kitchen for more water. He stops at the answering machine.

The first message is from the music critic of *The Jerusalem*

Post. The deep voice grates. "We would like to meet you, Mr. Sahne. Call us so you can be interviewed. Please call soon because later we may be too busy."

The next message is a familiar whispery voice. "Maestro Sahne, I suddenly find myself at the King David Hotel. I hope you are in town. Please come see me soon—that is, if your schedule permits."

In the King David suite, Gloria X, dressed in abundant pink silk, is seated in one of her winged chairs. She motions him to the other. This time her seraph seems to carry her above the domes and minarets of the Old City.

"It is a little extravagance of mine to bring my angels when I travel, but I find them so comforting. Usually I only bring one, not the pair, but I thought it would be rude not to have one for you in case you should come visit." She stretches an arm along a wing of the chair, revealing a floating gossamer sleeve.

"I hope it is all right to ask about the opera. You must absolutely tell me if I shouldn't be asking."

"I just wrote a note to you this morning but didn't get a chance to mail it." He hands it to her. Her lips move silently.

"Ah, the Shekhinah, the Shekhinah. I knew if you wrote an opera you would find a part for the Shekhinah, even before you had the idea. One could never tire of such a creature, could one?"

She looks at Sahne.

"No. Never. Speaking of creatures, did you bring your beautiful cats with you?"

"No. It's been very sad. Worrying and waiting all the time for their fragile hearts to give out became unbearable. I had to put them all to sleep."

Sahne has to catch his breath. He feels like he's been struck on the chest.

Gloria X cocks her head and smiles at him. "Now, dear Maestro, what do you do with your time when you're not composing?"

It takes him a moment to answer.

"I'm always composing somehow. Tonight I am going to the Wall. It is the great fast of Tisha B'Av. I remember going with my grandfather the summer I spent here after my mother died. I thought that seeing again the enormous crowds gathering to commemorate the destruction of the First and Second Temples might give me some ideas for the opera. It is, after all, this unrequited, unending longing that brought about the whole upheaval of Shabbatai Ṣevi. And it is said that the Shekhinah, too, waits and mourns for Her people at the site of the destroyed Temples."

Gloria X sits upright and leans forward in her chair, urgently, in a pose of intimacy although their chairs are actually separated by at least ten feet.

"Maestro, I have not been in a crowd for so long. May I ask a favor? You must deny me if you wish. I would love to go with you tonight, if only to observe the creative process. Would I be an inconvenience? May I come with you, please? Of course you must say no if I would disturb you, but I hope you will not refuse."

"I'd be happy to take you."

Sahne meets Gloria X in front of the King David. It is twilight and the air has begun to cool. Crowds are already converging along the streets toward the Old City. Gloria X wears a long white linen dress. Her blond hair is hidden, wrapped in a pale green turban. They get into her limousine. There is a rare, fleeting fragrance of violets. Sahne notices a second car, a sedan that follows them closely.

They enter the Old City at Zion Gate, slowly driving inside the perimeter wall. Their limousine glides through a sea of people, old and young, men and women, walking the same route.

"I remember this from when I was a teenager. The vast humanity. It doesn't after all seem like mourning, but some celebration."

"It is indeed very fascinating, Maestro. And, as you say, celebratory."

They stop at the entrance to the vast plaza around the Wall and walk through the military checkpoint. Two men get out of the sedan that has been following them. The men separate; one walks immediately ahead of them, the other behind. Sahne, Gloria X, and her bodyguards are buoyed gently here and there by the tides of the crowd.

Gloria X smiles at Sahne. "It is a bit overwhelming, this crowd, though I feel somehow absolutely free. Yes, free! May I take your hand, Maestro? It is such a fine hand. I noticed that when I met you—a musician's hand. I will be delicate. My hands are so large." She holds up her free hand and shows him. Sahne is surprised at its size, the broad palm, the thick fingers. He had not noticed before. She shakes her head gently. "My unfortunate hands have caused me great pain and made me self-conscious. My mother was ashamed of them. 'Hide your hands, darling,' she would always say. 'You have such peasant hands.' My own daughter had beautiful hands like yours, and she used them to take her own life. I'm sorry. I promised I wouldn't talk about her."

They move slowly through the crowd. Above them search-lights sweep back and forth, drawing strange hieroglyphics across the crowd and the stone buildings that surround the vast plaza. Sahne looks up and sees in the distance, standing high on the edge of the Wall, a small woman dressed in black robes. He turns to Gloria X to point out the figure. But when they look up together, she is gone. He hears a distant murmuring in the crowd and thinks perhaps the woman has suddenly jumped onto the worshipers standing below the Wall. The murmuring in the crowd grows closer and louder. Sahne is pulled away from Gloria X by a wave that moves through the crowd and tries to knock him down. He panics. He holds her hand tightly. "Mrs. X, don't let go!"

"What is happening, Maestro Sahne? Oh, my arm, my arm! It's going to break!"

He has to let go. He sees for a moment the heads of the bodyguards surrounding her, whirling about, escorting her away. Amazingly, they part the sea of people, making a space for her. He can see her moving away, though she is trying desperately to look back for him. One of the guards holds a walkie-talkie to his mouth with his free hand. Through its static, Sahne can hear her low, hoarse cry fading into the tumult. "Why, we must not leave Mr. Sahne. Oh my, goodbye, Maestro, good—"

Suddenly, ten feet in front of him, he sees a familiar profile. Isn't it the beautiful face from the Mamillah Pool? He feels a great relief and the beginning of joy. Since he came home that afternoon and heard Gloria X's message, he hadn't had time to think of the beautiful young man. He wants to call out above the screams that rise from the crowd, but he hesitates for a moment trying to remember his name.

"Hey! Hey! Sami!"

The young man turns to him. Alexander has been mistaken, it is someone else. People are screaming now, trying to move away as the man makes his way to Sahne. Sahne freezes. In the sudden sweep of a helicopter floodlight, he sees, pointed toward him, the blade of a knife.

And just as suddenly a hand emerges from the crowd, grabbing the knife, twisting it back, and plunging it into the assailant's heart.

When Sahne arrives at his apartment, it seems he has walked back from the Old City for hours in a daze. He cannot recall what happened after the crowd began kicking the murderer's crumpled and dying body. And he cannot recall what happened to his sports jacket. A sleeve is missing. The sole of one of his shoes is split. There is blood on his shirt. He feels slowly, gently, all along his chest and abdomen and around his neck, but there are no wounds.

His answering machine is blinking. There are two messages. Had he forgotten to erase the messages from earlier in the day? Again he hears the nagging voice from *The Jerusalem Post*.

"Have you received my message? Call us so you can have your interview. Next week we may be too busy."

The next message is frantic, shrill, loud.

"Oh, my God, Maestro Sahne, call me at once! I cannot bear waiting. I cannot stay in this place much longer! You must be alive! You must not leave me!"

And then he hears another voice, not shrill, but clear, luminous, ascendant.

He turns around.

And so the Shekhinah appears in a vision in the hallway of Opa Jacob's apartment, from the darkened doorway of the studio.

She appears to Alexander as She does to all who truly love Her.

She appears to Alexander as She had appeared to Ṣevi when he stood before the Sultan ready for martyrdom.

She commands him:

Stay in life.
Stay.
For here is My dominion.
Oh, My Beloved, We must never be separated.

New Memories

"The front is the back and the back is the front, because the side of the cottage facing the lake is called the front even if it looks like the back."

Mother's cousin Blossom, whom my sister and I had never seen before, arrived the summer after Father died, like a breeze off the water: cool, delicious, noisy in the trees.

"You know, kids, I spent plenty of summers here with your mother when I was growing up, when it was still your grandparents' place."

The lake is at its highest level in years. The branches of our willow hang down beyond a thin crescent of sand.

"This poor willow is weeping right into the lake, and do you two kids know why?"

We do not.

"Because her sweetheart is gone. Do you see any boy willows nearby?"

Blossom points for us. The closest willow is two cottages away. "Well, children, I rest my case."

Blossom shows us how to weave wreaths and crowns, necklaces and bracelets from the branches.

"Now, Sarah," Blossom says to my sister who is five, "you should wear your hair up like this, through this beautiful emerald tiara. That's it! Hold your head up high like a queen!"

Blossom isn't as religious as we are. She turns on lights on Saturdays, and she doesn't say a blessing before she eats. But she is always talking about people in the Bible.

"Last night I dreamed I was Queen Esther and soaked myself in fine oils and spices for months and months, though I know I would break out terribly if I did, not to mention going out of my mind."

Later in the kitchen, Sarah and Blossom make a beauty formula out of corn oil and sugar. Paprika is added for "tone and color," but they pour the whole mixture away because it smells bad.

Blossom says she has come over a thousand miles to the lake to help keep Mother company now that our poor father is gone. "She's as lonely as the willow. I haven't seen her since before she got married. That's eight years, and Alexander's already seven."

Now that Father is gone, Mother is thinking of selling the cottage she inherited from her parents. She is talking to Blossom in the kitchen. She brushes a strand of black hair from her cheek. "Sometimes it makes me sad. There are too many memories here."

"Make new memories," Blossom says.

Father is sitting up in the sunroom of our house in Windsor. It is a clear spring day. This is my favorite room, because there are large windows on three sides and on good days it is always bright. Even now, a broad shaft of sunlight has cut Father into triangles; the one that includes his head is bright, hazy, ghostly, the other, with a plaid blanket covering his lap, knees, and legs, is dark and shadowy.

"Alexander, can you tell the difference between a crocodile and an alligator?" Nowadays Father's voice is also ghostlike. I want to go outside and play but instead I bring him some paper and a pen. He draws for me. The crocodile has wide broad jaws, while the alligator has a narrow, elegant, and therefore more devious snout.

"Alexander, most people can't tell the difference between things. People only see what they know."

Blossom is fair-skinned with pale green eyes. All summer she wears shorts, a swimming top, and wooden sandals that go click-clop against her slightly yellowed heels. She always looks for shade. When we go for a walk along the country road, she wears a broad straw hat. "Milk turns quickly in the sun," she says.

Blossom likes to make up names for the flowers that grow in the narrow garden along our gravel driveway or in wild clusters along the road: fragile pink Jennie-May-Nots, gaping orange Last Laughs, small blue-and-violet Devil's Eyes.

"Adam and Eve named all the flowers in the Garden of Eden," she says. Blossom places a drooping red Grandfather's Tongue in Sarah's hair. "One day you'll be a grandmother!"

Mother is very quiet this summer. Often she sits on the swing bench that faces the lake. When we bring her bouquets of wildflowers that Blossom tells us to gather for her, she looks at us dreamily, caresses our hair, and smiles. Later Blossom tells us she is looking for traces of our father. "Children are like souvenirs," Blossom says, "mementos of love."

"The lake is a living creature just like us. If you listen to the waves, you can hear it breathing."

Blossom is showing Sarah and me how to dig up clumps of gray clay in the shallow water. "God made Adam out of clay," she says.

Later we are sitting on the dock forming passengers for Noah's Ark. Sarah is making gray bloblike cows. Blossom says they look like amoebas and are very lovely.

"Those are wonderful alligators, Alexander."

"These are crocodiles." I try to explain the difference, the length and breadth of the jaws, the shape of the tail.

"Well"—Blossom laughs—"it doesn't make much difference once you're in its stomach."

Blossom is making a figure of Mrs. Noah in a long dress

like a wedding gown. Mrs. Noah is too tall and thin at the waist to stand up and keeps drooping over.

"She'll have to dry out and harden before she can stand," Blossom says. "She's supposed to be a beautiful woman. Love makes a woman beautiful. Your mother and I are both thirty-two, and I hate to admit it, but your mother's more beautiful because she had your father's love.

"Did you kids know that I introduced them, sort of? I used to go out with your father before he met your mother. The first time he saw her he was smitten!"

Mother and Blossom are looking through the picture album. Father is hanging upside down from a tree branch next to mother. His dark hair is a triangle pointing to the ground.

"He was so handsome and he sure had a great sense of humor," Blossom is saying, "even though he was the serious type."

Mother smiles and gives a little laugh. When she laughs it is as if she has awakened from a long trance.

"Well, I have to admit I was always jealous of you," Blossom says, "I found him first, remember?"

"Yes, Blossom, of course I do."

One night, Blossom comes into our room.

"Alexander . . . Sarah . . . wake up. Shoosh . . . don't wake Mother. Tonight's the night to gather moons. First we'll need some traps."

We follow her into the kitchen in our pajamas without turning on the lights.

"Pots and pans are best," she says, "so are the bowls."

The screen door screeches as we slip outside. We each carry a few rattling traps as we head for the dock.

"He's riding high and proud tonight," she says looking up at the bright dish of moon over the lake.

Blossom leans out over the dock's edge. In the moonlight, through her nightdress, I can see the shadow of her breasts with their little tips pointing to the water. One by one she fills the pots, pans, and bowls.

"Look, you caught a minnow!" Sarah claps, looking into the salad bowl.

"That means good luck, kids!"

"Good luck!" we repeat.

We arrange the traps along the edges of the dock. Blossom shows us how each one catches a reflection of the moon if we look at the proper angle.

"A moon is not an easy thing to hold on to, kids."

Next morning when Mother sees all the pots and pans and bowls lying in the drainboard, she laughs. "Out catching moons, Blossom?"

The lake cottage is half an hour from Windsor, where we live during the year and where Mother and Blossom both grew up. Now that Blossom is "in the neighborhood," she is calling up an old boyfriend.

"Mickey! Guess who! . . . You still recognize my voice after all these years? Fine . . . At the lake with my cousins . . . She's doing fine considering. . . . Well, you know, Windsor got too small for me. When you coming out to Vancouver?"

Blossom is holding the telephone receiver between her shoulder and cheek. She is carefully painting her toenails with Summer Passion polish. Her slender foot turns this way and that.

Later Blossom says that Mickey Segal wanted to marry her a long time ago but she wasn't in love with him though he's a nice guy. Now Mickey Segal owns the biggest hardware store in Windsor and is very rich. "He still hasn't gotten over me in all these years!" Blossom says.

Mickey Segal still isn't married. The next evening he arrives at the cottage to take Blossom out to dinner and a movie. He is a little shorter than Blossom, who for the occasion is wearing a sleeveless blue sundress and her usual wooden sandals. Mickey Segal is starting to go bald.

"Au revoir . . . Adiós!" Blossom waves at us as Mickey helps her into a big silver car with tailfin lights.

I wake up late at night when they drive up the gravel driveway. They walk around to the front and sit in the swing bench watching the lake and talking quietly. Nothing is happening, so I go back to sleep.

"We saw that new Marilyn Monroe movie," Blossom is telling my mother at breakfast while they are having their coffee. "You could see right through her dress!"

"Mickey said that my figure was better than hers. I said, 'Mickey, you haven't changed. You were always given to exaggeration.' Well anyway, it would never work. I hate hardware."

⚓

At the end of August we are driving into Windsor to take Blossom to the train station. The city always looks strange near the end of summer. It is so bright and hot and quiet, like a desert town.

Blossom says she cannot leave until she makes her farewell prophecies. "Sarah is going to be the most beautiful girl in the world and marry the richest man in Canada. Alexander will be wise and handsome like his father. Anyway, I'll see you all before then.

"The children will make you happy again," she says, turning to my mother.

When Blossom gets on the train I begin to cry but I pretend not to. I turn around as if I have something in my eye. I did not even cry when my father died or at his funeral or during the week of mourning when people came by and said things like, "Well, now you'll have to help take care of your mother and sister," or, "Now you are the big little man in the family." I had wandered through those days watching all around me as if I could live and breathe and never have to feel.

THE SEAT OF
HIGHER CONSCIOUSNESS

The night of the coup, Zahava travels far and wide. She flies over lush mountain valleys and Babel-like ruins. She hovers in the mist above vast primordial waters. In the morning, she awakens with a shudder and begins to recite the prayer "I have dreamed a dream and do not know its meaning" when her telephone rings.

"Chaos—that's our real enemy," the woman from the State Department is saying, "but we're working to find him. We won't give up until every American is released. We can assure you of that."

And then, after coming downstairs to the living room and switching on CNN, Zahava sees tanks rumbling down a Central American esplanade, clustering around the pink, bullet-marked presidential palace.

Zahava is her brother's contact. She handles all his business: confidential government mailings, income tax forms, overseas bank account statements, credit card payments—mostly for foreign restaurants and hotels. She keeps Ehud's will in her desk drawer. She has a closet full of his extra clothes.

"Zahava, Zahava," she hears him saying, telephoning from this latest assignment, "you're in exile from the living world. *Va'taytzay*," he continues, switching to the dense, ancient syntax, the allusive language of archetypal predicaments. *"And she went out of the place,"* as it is written of Naomi in Moab and by which Zahava understands he means, "Come visit me in this new place, Zahava. You need to get away from all that tragedy and do some traveling."

Her father is out attending morning services. He contemplates the letter *mem* that begins the *Ma Tovu* ("How Goodly Are Your Dwelling Places") and then continues through the weekday liturgy, the added prayers of the New Moon, concluding with, since it is Friday morning, the *mem sofit*—the altered *mem* as it appears, closed, boxlike, contrite, at the end of *yamim*, the final word of the Ninety-third Psalm—"Holiness becomes Thy House, O Lord, for the length of days."

Zahava helps her mother from the bed to the bathroom, settling her in the special shower chair. Zahava's slight figure, dressed for work and protected by a blue plastic apron, flutters attentively with the spray attachment about the heavy, naked body. Zahava frequently confronts her father. "All the junk food you give her is making her obese, it's so unhealthy," to which he smiles and replies, "Zahava, our slender one, why deny Mother her pleasures?"

Her mother gives herself obediently to Zahava's care. "Mommy, lift your arm this way. Yes, slowly, that's good." She dries her with a soft towel, then dresses her in a clean pink linen dress. She is about to serve her mother breakfast when her father returns.

He comes through the house in a halo of winter air. "Zahava, do you know what? I've been thinking all morning about the letter *mem*. And it's been a revelation!"

She stops him in the living room. "Father, please listen." She tells him about the coup, the State Department call. He stands still, staring at his outstretched fingers. "Where does this come from? I look inward, and at your mother. What are these people and places to Ehud? They're outside our history. And all this flying—'It is not in the heavens!'"

Her father believes that the personalities of children are derived from facets of the parents. Ehud spoils his theories. In his earliest essay for *The Modern Traditionalist*, "A Differential Equation of Sons: Yacov and the Twelve Tribes," her father tries to trace each son's personality to a component, an action, even a spoken phrase of the patriarch. He brings proofs (most, in Zahava's opinion, quite weak) from ancient texts. "The spiritual world is an *aspaklariyah*," he concludes, inserting an Aramaic word found in the Talmud, "that is, a mirror of our physical world, and vice versa. So it stands to reason that the countless generations of souls must have their own replicating genetic strands, helical bands of a celestial substance." It has not occurred to him, as it does to Zahava, that new souls might form of their own accord, from the unseen breath of God, independent of corporeal laws, unpredictable as clouds.

Her father motions to the kitchen. He leans over and whispers in Zahava's ear, "You didn't tell Mother, I hope. God knows how it might upset her. Ehud's still her baby." He says this though her mother is long a broken husk, a shattered vessel, who spends her day sitting quietly, eyes roaming. Zahava remembers her on long-ago afternoons, coming up the front-porch steps after lecturing at the university, adjusting her skirt, her fine limbs swaying, or, in the evenings after dinner, humming in her study, leaning over her typewriter, smoothing back her dark hair with her hand.

"Come, Zahava, before you go to bed, help Mommy figure out the root of this word. It's a mystery to me. It has three consonants, see . . ." And another evening, sitting at her desk, which is covered with open books, her mother explains. "It's a funny thing this letter *vav,* this 'and' conversive, that changes future into past, and past to future. The Chumash is full of it, and so are the preceding texts of the Ugarits." She points to a line in Genesis. "For example, the passage regarding Joseph and Potiphar's wife, 'And he left his garment in her hand and fled,' is really constructed in what we nowadays consider the future tense, 'he will leave his garment in her hand, he will flee,' but the 'and' converts them to the past. It is a riddle that reflects, after all, a different, more simultaneous concept of time, mysterious even to us, the descendants. This is what your mother stuffs her head with! Well, Zahava, *t'huzahavi.*" She conjugates her daughter's name using biblical rules. She is, in her own way, blessing Zahava, saying, "You shall be all gold!"

Just then her brother comes into the study dressed in pajamas. He is ten. Zahava is twelve. Although he is two years younger, the child Ehud is taller than Zahava. His features are fine and handsome, his hair black and thick. Zahava is small and plain, her head slightly narrow. But she is proud of Ehud's beauty, as if it reflects on her in some way, as the moon delights in the sun.

Often her mother answers the exclamations of some adult visitor, "Yes, I know, Ehud, our baby, is a beautiful boy, but Zahava has a higher beauty—she is 'tender-eyed,' as it is written of Leah, and, as her name implies, has a golden soul. Perhaps that's why God protected her. She's a living miracle, you know. She was only two pounds, four ounces when she was born!"

Her mother now hugs her gently by the shoulders as Ehud approaches. "Look, Zahava. *'V'hayonah*—and the dove found no rest for the sole of its foot and returned to them in the ark.'"

Ehud smiles, looking eagerly, wide-eyed at his mother. "Now, conjugate my name!"

"Ah, Ehud. I was just getting to that, wasn't I, Zahava?" And in a singsong she continues, *"Ahud ima, ahud olam*—Mother's beloved, beloved of the world!"

In the afternoon their mother goes in her car to the university. She is teaching one course in the summer session. Zahava and Ehud are playing in the backyard, a large grassy area with an ancient oak in the far corner. Ehud moves a small shoe box on an old pulley clothesline suspended from the back porch to the tree. "A monorail," he says. He captures some ants and carefully puts them in the box for passengers. "I haven't learned it yet, Zahava. What's their Hebrew name?"

Zahava is proud of her vocabulary. Her mother says it is outstanding. "*Nimoloh* is one ant, singular. *Nimoliym* is plural."

Her brother sings to the traveling ants and plays a simple word game, "*Nimoliym, nimoliym,* your root-tee-root-toot-toot *is nun, mem, lamed.*"

"That's pretty good, Ehud."

"Look, Zahava, the *nimoliym* are visiting Disneyland!"

They hear the phone ringing. Their father, pale and bewildered, comes out through the flapping screen door. He mumbles something about staying near the house. And then he says, mostly to himself, it seems, "I'll be back soon with Mother. Yes, yes, I'll certainly be back with Mother."

Their father tries to prepare them. There has been a car accident. "Mother is still with us, but her soul is hidden, as when God hides His face from His people. But it's different, because Mother is not angry with us. And because her soul is within her, as the fruit is within its skin, she still knows and understands and loves us. Meanwhile we will have to take care of her physical needs, because that is the requirement of love."

When their mother comes home several months later, it seems to Zahava as if one endless day has passed, a *yoma arichta,* a long day when wondrous species are created or whole worlds destroyed; an eternal, solemn, holy day as long as an epoch.

A ramp has been built alongside the front-porch stairs. When the hospital attendants, three short and heavy men, bring their mother home, they ignore the new ramp and carry her up the stairs, placing her wheelchair down in the front hall.

Her mother's limbs are bony, her wide eyes move strangely this way and that. She scratches herself immodestly. Zahava is too horrified to cry. She feels herself filling up with a hard and cold sadness. Ehud simply glances into the front hall and retreats. Zahava follows him into the living room. Seeing him standing there expressionless, she cannot think of what to say. And then she remembers and whispers, *"Ahud ima, ahud olam."*

Ehud looks silently down at his hands and walks out of the room.

That night her father tells Zahava how he met his wife in college. Her father, already ordained but leery of a rabbinical post, is studying mathematics and philosophy. Her mother studies ancient Near Eastern languages and comparative linguistics.

"Why linguistics?" her father asks the tall, dark-haired young woman whom providence seats next to him in the library.

"Because the sages say, and I believe, the world is incarnated from words."

"I fell in love with her then," her father says, looking at his wife in her wheelchair.

And so Zahava knows how one might create a world of sacrifice, a sphere of duty, from some fine words somebody says, some flare of magic they produce.

Days later, Zahava stands and peers into her mother's placid eyes. "Mommy, Mommy. Hello, Mommy." Her mother blinks slowly. Her father walks into the room. Zahava thinks he might be upset, but he speaks earnestly, "Zahava, our golden one, what do you see in there? What do you see?"

She has no answer.

Now, after she has told her father that Ehud is missing, he solemnly asks Zahava, "Are you going to teach this morning?"

Yes. She is. She sees no reason to stay home. She has given the State Department her phone number at school. The woman will call if there is news. When you teach small children you must never be late or unreliable. Children, a famous *maggid* has said, are like the delicate bulrushes that protected baby Moses in the Nile. They are easily damaged. If we are not careful, they may be bent and broken by our habits.

When Zahava enters the classroom, the children stand up briefly and greet the teacher, "Good morning, *morah*." They stand up again when the principal, Rabbi Flucht, a young, bearded man, peeks in the doorway. He disappears and they tumble back into their seats. Zahava raises a thin arm in the air, and the children sing as if just awakening from sleep:

"*Modeh Ani,* I am grateful to You, Everlasting King,
  Who returns each morning my soul in mercy."

During the first months her mother is home, Zahava's father walks around exhausted, with the bewildered look that has settled in on him. They are unable to keep a nurse or a companion for long, because her father is always haranguing them. "My wife's not comfortable in that position," he says, or, "She really shouldn't be sitting in front of that window, it's way too sunny," or, "Nurse, I think my wife's hungry again. I can tell when my wife is hungry." Her mother never speaks, but once, in the middle of the night, Zahava hears a frail voice through the wall that separates her room from her parents': "What is it? What is it?"

And her father's voice answers, "Everything's fine, Malka. Everything's fine. You'll be better soon. I'll always take care of you."

Her father leaves his post at the university and takes a position at a local community college. The pay and prestige are less but the hours are better, the demands fewer. "I was on tenure track, but those things don't matter much after all," her father says. "And besides, I won't have to worry about publishing academic papers. I can write my essays about what interests me—that is, when I have some spare time. And I can help Mother with her work. Well, at least she's sleeping better now."

In his first essay from that period, "The Seat of Higher Consciousness," published in *The Well of Knowledge*, the magazine of the American Orthodox Congress, her father writes, "The soul is immanent in the body and yet, so to speak, separate therefrom, of a different dimension. Diseases and disorders of the corporeal brain do not disprove this sacred notion, as the materialists would have us believe, for in such situations the soul is merely temporarily restrained, as a prisoner may be held chained within his cell, looking out at the world through iron bars, until the day of God's redemption."

After the essay is published he is invited to speak at the annual convention of the congress, at their medical ethics forum. "I started out writing these essays for myself," he tells Zahava. "But it is a good feeling to influence people with one's ideas. I am humbly reminded of what Rava wrote to Rav Meir almost two millennia ago: "You are in Babylonia, but your nets are spread out in Jerusalem!'"

"*Shomartoh,* you watched, speaking to a boy. *Shomart,* you watched, speaking to a girl." Zahava translates the conjugations she writes out on the blackboard. She draws the three-consonant root of each verb in pink chalk, the vowel markings and ancillary consonants in blue. *Qal* is the simplest conjugation for the children to learn but still requires much repetition. The children write slowly in their notebooks in cursive script.

After his mother's accident, Ehud's Hebrew handwriting deteriorates. "Ehud," his father pleads, sitting with the squirming boy over his workbook, "if you pay more attention and practice, you won't make messy mistakes. Remember, you have your mother's genes and knack for language." But Ehud battles his consonants, the *shin* and *tzadi* roll over on their heads, the *gimmel* like a double agent mimics the *zayin.* The little comma-like *yud,* instead of hovering delicately in the air like a hummingbird, crashes to the bottom of the line. "I don't understand what the problem is," her father says to Zahava. "His English handwriting hasn't changed and is very neat. Why won't he write Hebrew nicely?"

Zahava tries to help, too. Before Passover, she says, "Let's make our own Haggadah, Ehud. We can write out all the words in fancy letters and decorate the pages with our own drawings."

"No."

"Zahava, Zahava! Ehud is home!" her father announces. Ehud rarely comes home from his out-of-state college.

Ehud asks his father and Zahava to sit down in the living room.

"*My* God, *my* redemption," Ehud begins, calm and serious, "is motion and change and flight." He then reveals that for the past three years he has gradually dropped all his college courses and, using his tuition money, has been taking extensive flying lessons.

"I just received my pilot's license. I'm getting a job in Africa. It's a small company and a small plane, but I can get some good flight experience to get the type of job I'd like."

Her father turns pale. "Africa? Doing what? I thought you liked college. . . . Flying where?"

"'That which has wings will tell the matter.'"

Her father sags in his chair. "Where does this come from? I can't believe this. Thank God your mother is in her room resting. It would kill her if she heard you were doing this."

Ehud grimaces.

Her father looks to Zahava for help. She sits, somber, her slender hands folded on her lap. Out of pity for their father she says to Ehud, "You could still go back to college. You still could finish." Zahava herself did not go to a university as her father had wished, but went to the Bais Yacov Teachers' Seminary. Here, too, her father had been opposed, dismayed.

The first time she tried to persuade him she said, "Teaching children is sacred, Father."

"Of course, but you could go to university, too. And I really insist you must. Our holy sages all knew the sciences and cultures of their day. There are many sacred roles in life. Remember, your mother is a professor and so am I. And, you know, we were hoping that if you shared your mother's interests, you could continue her work. I'm really not good at it. I've not advanced her ideas at all. Anyway, that would make her very happy. Doesn't that interest you?"

Now, sitting in the living room with Ehud and her father, Zahava waits, glancing from one to the other, but Ehud does not answer her.

"Zahava," her father finally asks, as if Ehud is no longer in the room, "did you know this was happening? Did he ever tell you? He is walking away, once and for all, from his history, not only from our lives. Do you know where this comes from?"

But Zahava does not know. For so many years Ehud has been distant from her, too. And, she believes, she does not and will never know where things come from; neither the mysterious grammar of God, nor the endless creation of souls.

Ehud gets up and approaches his sister. "I'm going now. Goodbye. I'll write to you." He bends over her seated figure and kisses her on the cheek. She is surprised by the warmth of his face, by the sudden affection. A thick lock of his hair brushes against her eyes. He whispers in her ear, "Don't spend your entire life in this house, Zahava." He turns and looks for a moment at their father, who is silently staring at his hands. "Goodbye, Father."

Ehud leaves the room. They hear the front door close. Her father stands up.

"That boy has thrown away the seed and kept the chaff. A crazy life!"

Her father believes that all inanimate things yearn for life. "Zahava, why do the continents move over the millennia? Why do the seas chase after the moon?" or "Zahavale, what is spoken by the blowing wind, or in the distant rumblings of the Earth? It is their prayer, their challenge, to God Almighty to become living things!"

He works this theme into a long essay, "The Hills Danced Like Rams," which is rejected by *The Modern Traditionalist* and even by the lesser organ of synthetic thought, *The Burning Bush.* The editor of *The Burning Bush,* who had gone with him to university, responds, "My dear and respected colleague: This crap is a sorry mishmash of Darwin and Spinoza! It's not even fresh. We cannot publish it. Try *Commonweal!*"

"'And Yacov went out . . . and he lighted upon the place,'" Zahava tells the children, as the great commentator Rashi explains, "means that distance contracted for him. Imagine, everyone"—she demonstrates by extending her thin leg— "stretching out your foot and traveling ten miles!" The children giggle in wonder. A little boy asks, "Was Yacov-Our-Father very tall?"

"Not particularly. Remember, this was a miracle!"

Zahava receives a letter from Ehud written on Nairobi Hilton stationery.

"I'm still looking for an apartment. Meanwhile the company is putting me up here. This is a very beautiful city high in the mountains. Guess what, I hear there is even a synagogue." He tells her the name of the company and some of the places where he flies, Chad, Somalia, Djibouti. He does not mention what he is transporting or why. He asks his sister to take care of a few things for him, check his bank statements, apply in his name for a telephone card. "Thanks for looking out for me," he concludes, then changes to his barely legible Hebrew script, *Zokharti lokh ḥesed n'urayikh*—"I remember the kindness of your youth, when you followed me in an unsown land." He encloses a picture of himself standing on a dusty runway, next to a small white airplane, in the company of several scrawny African soldiers. On the back is written, "My faithful guardians."

During her campaign to attend the Bais Yacov Teachers' Seminary and not a secular college, Zahava asks her father, "Isn't philosophy and even science unreliable? Scientists are always changing around their theories back and forth."

"That is a tautology."

She invokes steadfast faith. "But *emunah*—"

"Zahava. Now you sound like one of those fanatics who are afraid of any rational thought. Do you think I have no faith? We didn't raise you or educate you in religious schools for that, though clearly the Torah schools have been overrun by Neanderthals! Why, your mother and I . . . Well, never mind." He turns away from Zahava and goes to his study, closing the door behind him.

Later that evening he comes out and finds her reading in the living room. He taps her on the shoulder. "Of course, Zahava, you must do what your heart bids you. Your mother and I are very proud of you. How wonderful to teach children. Yes, how wonderful." He places his hands on her head and blesses her.

After Zahava graduates from the Bais Yacov Teachers' Seminary and is hired by Rabbi Flucht, her father has a new door put in the upstairs hallway that leads to her bedroom, an upstairs bathroom, and the spare bedroom. The spare bedroom is made into a sitting room so the whole area seems like a separate little apartment. A new telephone line is installed in Zahava's bedroom. "You are a young woman now, Zahava," her father says. "You should have a little privacy." But their lives become more intertwined. When Zahava comes down each morning to see her mother, she begins to notice that her hair is poorly combed, or that her clothes, though always clean, are beginning to wear. Zahava buys her new dresses in bright colors. She begins to share the tasks her father has always performed, the bathing and feeding of her mother.

"Zahava, you are building a great palace in Paradise with your deeds," her father says.

One evening he teases his daughter, finding her gently manicuring her mother's nails. "Let's see, by now your palace in Paradise should have solid-gold floors, ruby chandeliers, and, of course, diamond windows!"

"I have no interest in palaces."

Her father's eyes are downcast, he is trying not to cry. "Really, Zahava . . . you shouldn't be spoiling me or your mother. We're old-timers now. We've had our chance. What's happened to us has happened. It's not fair . . . to you. You have to begin your own life. If you even wanted to find your own place, and move out on your own, we would help you."

"*Reuven, Shimon, Levy, Yehuda . . .*" The children are singing a song to help them remember the twelve tribes. When they come to the last name, Binyomin, they clap their hands and sing all the names once more. "Music," Zahava's teacher in seminary would say, "is the handmaiden of Memory."

Ehud wins the Chumash memorization contests that are held each semester for the elementary students in their yeshiva day school. In this respect he is considered something of a prodigy. Ehud can close his eyes and recite whole chapters from the Bible. His father says he is like a cistern that retains every drop, and predicts he will be a great linguist like his mother. Ehud enjoys practicing in front of his mother and Zahava, who follow along in the text, checking on his grammar. He hardly makes mistakes. "*Bravo! Bravo! Perfetto!*" their mother says. And one time it occurs to her to ask, "So what's your secret, Ehud sweetheart? Do you have a photographic memory? Do you see the words when you close your eyes?"

The boy shrugs his shoulders. "Sort of. It's like I'm walking through the rooms of our house and reading what I've scribbled on the walls."

Her mother is astonished and runs to her husband, who is watching the television news. "My God, Yacov, he's stumbled into Ricci's *Memory Palace!*"

Rabbi Flucht, the principal of the day school, does not approve of television sets. "It's like putting a sewer pipe in the middle of your living room," he often tells the children at assembly. "Would you do that?" He speaks very softly, enchanting the children. They always giggle. And to Zahava he says with a smile—he knows his best young teacher is a daughter of one of those "other" rabbis, rabbis with Ph.D.'s, weak-faithed souls obsessed with reconciling man's illusory knowledge with the reality of God's law—"Zahava," he whispers after one of the assemblies, "you're a modern woman. I'm sure in your home you get every possible channel."

"I agree with you in principle, Rabbi Flucht, but nowadays we need to know what's going on in the world. I know there's not much I could do for my brother if there were a problem, but I feel it's a matter of *pekuaḥ nefesh*"—she uses the legal term for endangered lives, for whom most laws are suspended.

"Oh, yes. I was just teasing. By the way, Zahava, would you like to meet my wife's brother? He's a fine young man."

She says she would like to, but it might be difficult just now because of her family obligations.

At Friday-evening meal, their father's eyes suddenly widen in amazement. A morsel of fish hangs perilously on the fork he holds frozen in midair in front of their mother. Their mother's mouth remains open, waiting. "Perhaps," their father says, "the World to Come is composed of real physical elements, the so-called dark matter, proposed by some modern physicists, that we cannot see or measure. A sort of modern version of the ethers or vortices." Their father is about to resume feeding his wife when Ehud, his dinner untouched, abruptly rises from the table. His chair tips over with a thud. He does not bother to set it back up, and walks out of the room.

"Well"—her father gets up and rights the fallen chair, still holding the fish-laden fork—"we clearly have evidence that invisible forces such as gravity exist, so we should make our own deductions, and thereby strengthen our *emunah*, our steadfast faith—"

"But Father," Zahava interrupts. It bothers her more and more that he does not let her mother feed herself. "The Torah regards scientific knowledge with indifference."

Her father sits back down. "Have you been reading that Leibowitz book? You know I don't agree with him. He's a cantankerous old man. Everything that happens and everything God creates, even scientific laws, must have a meaning for us, if only we are willing to look for it."

❧

Six months after Ehud's arrival in East Africa, Zahava receives a phone call from Curaçao. "I'm working around the Caribbean basin now. The job came up all of a sudden. Better pay and connections. It's beautiful here, Zahava, come visit me when I'm settled in. I may be receiving some mail from the State Department at home, and from the United Nations Special Services. Would you please forward it all to this address?"

She tells her father. "It all sounds very important."

"Something's missing, Zahava. We have no idea what he's doing."

"Well, he sounds happy. We should not judge him. If it has to do with the State Department and the UN, it can't be so bad."

"This world is a *prozdor.*" Her father, quoting the Chapters of the Fathers, uses the Aramaic word for "vestibule."

"This world is *this* world," Ehud says sullenly. He has just finished ninth grade and announces that he will not go back to the yeshiva day school he has attended with Zahava since childhood. "I've had enough of that. Next year I'm going to public school. I just want to make it clear."

"We can't permit it."

"Well, I don't care. I'm going to public school or no school." Ehud's voice is disturbingly calm. He can do that, Zahava thinks. Lately he can say upsetting things with no emotion, almost with indifference. Zahava does not know why, but it makes her blush.

"Think of how your mother will feel. It's not our world."

Ehud turns away and goes up to his room.

Zahava knocks twice on the door, but he doesn't answer. In the fall he attends public school.

The principal returns to Zahava's class. On Friday mornings, Rabbi Flucht gives a Chumash contest and asks the children questions. They write down their answers on a sheet of paper. That morning he asks: Who are the wives of Lemech? Where is Rachel buried, and why is she buried there? We all know from the Torah that the moon was created equal to the sun. What was the sin of the moon that caused her to be diminished?

The prize for the most correct answers is usually a book, but today it is a toy, a fluorescent spinning top, which he takes out of his pocket and hands to the winner. "Good work, David. A studious boy deserves to play, too."

After class, Flucht comes up to Zahava in the hallway. "Isn't your brother working in that country with the coup? God Almighty, where is that place exactly?"

Ehud covers the walls of his room with colored maps of the world, textured diagrams of the ocean floor, gray-black charts of the moon, star-studded expanses of the universe.

"Ehud," Zahava hears her father saying to the boy, "do you know that God created and destroyed hundreds of worlds before he created this one? Think of all those maps!"

Ehud's interest in maps is reflected in his favorite books, which stand neatly on his bookcase, *The Sun and Planets,* the Britannica *Atlas of the Earth,* Cousteau's *The Ocean World.*

Though he daily refers to these books, every night before bed they are carefully returned to their places on the bookshelves. He does not allow the housekeeper to enter his room. "I can keep it clean myself."

When Ehud starts public school, Zahava stops her habit of peeking into his room to say good night. It seems to Zahava that now that Ehud has changed schools, his very being, the habitation of his soul, has been removed to a distant geography.

After Curaçao, Ehud works for six months in Cambodia. His father says to Zahava, "This is more unbelievable than Africa!"

Ehud writes Zahava a letter that is postmarked from Thailand: "I had to send this with the United Nations courier to Bangkok. There is no reliable mail service here. I am grateful that you are good enough to never ask questions. I myself don't have many answers, but my work is always on the up-and-up. We are subcontracting for the UN."

When he leaves Cambodia six months later, he phones Zahava from somewhere over the Pacific. His voice is surprisingly clear. "The company decided to pull out—*va'timoleh*—if you know what I mean." And she understands, in that heavily affixed biblical work, how even now, as in ancient times, the earth is filled with violence.

"Thank you for filling out those tax forms," he continues. "I'm moving on to Central America. I'll call you when I'm settled. I'll be close enough for you to visit."

Zahava comes home at lunchtime. The secular subjects of the dual curriculum are taught by others in the afternoon.

Her father is watching television in the living room. Her mother is sitting nearby in the reclining lounge chair, her eyes fixed on a cold fireplace. A small particle of cottage cheese from lunch sticks to her upper lip. Annoyed, Zahava takes a napkin from the coffee table and gently wipes her mother's lip. "Really, Father, you should be more—"

"Oh, it's okay," her father whispers, motioning to the television. A commercial is now playing. "They haven't mentioned a single name, let alone Ehud's, except for some spoiled journalist who's been imprisoned in his luxury suite at the Sheraton. He's not allowed to leave his room but can order room service. I can't imagine a son of mine would be caught up in this confusion. Anyway, Mother is always bored by news programs." He stretches his arms forward. "It's a crazy world down there, Zahava. First they reported the president was killed, and then it was announced that he was alive and had been flown by helicopter to his house in the countryside to await his loyal troops. And then there are rumors that our military might get involved because we have bases down there, and that's why the rebels kidnapped so many Americans—"

"Father, look, the commercial is over."

A reporter at the Hotel Intercontinental, across the street from the Presidential Palace, is demonstrating the portable satellite dish he is using to transmit his report. "The coup leaders have shut down all the country's broadcasting facilities." When the reporter adjusts the small metal cone, the sun's reflection flashes across the street, startling Zahava.

Her mother's paper, "'And' in the Time of the Ugarits and Early Semites," is accepted by *Natural Linguistics* just before her accident but is not published until two years later. The delay is due to the minor revisions requested, which Zahava's father takes over a year to complete.

"It's hard to think like your mother. She's an original. I had to be careful or she'd have been upset," her father explains.

The day the new journal arrives in the mail, he grabs hold of Zahava's hands and whirls her across the living room. "A day of dancing and gladness!" He swings the journal up in the air. Its blue-and-white cover shines in the room light. He places the open magazine in his wife's lap. "Look, Malka, it's even the lead article!" Her mother sits indifferently in her chair. She closes her eyes.

"Well, she's just very tired now," he says to Zahava. "She'll be very pleased when I tell her again later."

In the introduction her mother writes, "All time is simultaneous to the ancient mind, that which *has been* and that which is fated *to be.* Those are the Perfect and Imperfect dreams of a language developed before the philosophical adornments of Free Will."

Her father does the cooking for the Friday-night meal. "I'd better go in the kitchen and start preparing for dinner. You look tired, Zahava. Go upstairs and take a nap. I'll keep you posted."

Eyes closed, lying on her bed, Zahava sees her children's faces, the black-on-white print of their Bibles and commentaries. She sees their notebooks, the box-shaped letters now marching, now tumbling off the pale blue lines. She floats through her house, holding Ehud's hand. They are reading from the Torah—the words are scrolled upon the walls. The wives of Lemech come before her: Ada, who has borne her husband's children, and Zilah, who has drunk the cup of barrenness to preserve her beauty. They point and laugh at the diminished moon, who has angered God by complaining, "How can two sovereigns rule the sky?" The moon is falling on Zahava's head. She awakens.

When Zahava comes downstairs for dinner, her father says, "I'll just leave the television on in the living room so we don't have to touch the switch." That way they will not violate the oncoming Sabbath. "I'll just tell Mother later that I forgot to shut it off, so she doesn't get suspicious."

Usually Zahava's mother has her dinner with them, but this evening she seems tired and keeps closing her eyes. Her father lets his wife sleep in the recliner chair in the living room while they eat in the dining room. "I'll give her dinner later when she wakes up. She'll be hungry then." Zahava stands while her father sings "A Woman of Virtue" in praise of his wife and then as he makes the benediction over the wine. In the background they hear the drone of the television in the living room.

They sit down. Zahava and her father quietly pass each other the platters of food.

"Well, during the first days," her father says, as if he were continuing a conversation—he is cutting into a piece of roast chicken without looking up—"in those terrible days, it flickered on the windowsill *between* the bands of sunlight that came through the venetian blinds. It shimmered on the intravenous bag. Of course, it's not something you could easily prove you saw to a nonbeliever. It was really like an altered frequency of light. Other times, I knew, by a peculiar electricity in the air, that it waited, nervous and frightened, near the fluorescent light above your mother's bed. And then, a few days later, I knew Mother would live for sure—I knew before the doctors did, and they were very pessimistic, though I never told you or Ehud—because one day your mother's *neshamah* ceased its peregrinations in the room and settled back, may God be forever praised, into its corporeal home."

Her father shrugs and continues eating dinner silently. Zahava feels cold and shivery. After grace her father insists on clearing the table himself and doing the dishes.

Zahava goes to the living room.

The same reporter as earlier is standing in front of the Hotel Intercontinental. "Our sources indicate that the coup is collapsing. The sudden quiet on the streets is eerie." He goes on to explain that the military is disproportionately split, with only a minority supporting the coup. Some of the coup leaders have been shot by troops loyal to the president.

The reporter presses his earphone to his ear. "We have some important, late-breaking news." They switch to another reporter standing in a large conference room at an undisclosed air base. She is wearing army fatigues.

"A group of missing Americans working on government contracts has just arrived from the jungle where they had been abducted by supporters of the coup. We are told they were abandoned by their captors and wandered all day without food or clean water until American helicopters picked them up. Here they come."

A dozen or so bedraggled young men are now filing into the large room. Zahava wants to call out to her father but is afraid to move, even to breathe. She does not see Ehud. One man points to the bandage covering the side of his face and says something to the reporter that Zahava cannot understand. Cameras in the room flash and click.

And then she sees him. Out of the corner of the camera's eye. Ehud. Alive. Next to the other Americans in the room, he seems short, exhausted, weak. He turns to the camera and she knows he is looking for her. "Father, Father! Come quick!" she calls out, but the scene lasts only an instant, and a news anchor in Washington is already on the screen.

"What is it? What is it?"

Zahava feels a pale illumination in the room, a brief electrification. Has her mother actually spoken? She turns around.

Her mother is sitting in her recliner chair, eyes closed. The phone begins ringing in Zahava's bedroom. She knows it must be the State Department, but she feels no need to run up and answer it.

Her father comes into the room. "Has anything happened? Zahavale, what happened?"

For a long moment Zahava cannot speak. Her father turns pale. He presses his hands, two clenched fists, to his chest.

"Ehud is alive, Father," she says in wonder.

She wants now only to weep—endlessly—as Rachel weeps outside Bethlehem, for her own lonely sojourn, and for her children who march past her grave into exile.

Zahava stares quietly, dry-eyed, unseeing, at the television screen, though she needs so desperately to weep—for all of the children in everlasting time, compelled like their mother to wander forever in a wandering world.

THE CREATION OF ANAT

Anat boarded the train. Carefully, avoiding strain, she settled in a window seat to view the great river that would appear at the outskirts of the city, curving and stretching deep into the summer country. In the months since she completed her anatomic atlas, a grinding labor of twelve years, a rare virus had entered her heart, weighing down her tall, thin frame. Even Dr. Konig, the chairman of the Institute, noticed. He had stood in the doorway of her laboratory, his fat chin hanging.

"Why, you are stooping, my dear. Remember, you are the Empress of Embryology! The loveliest jewel in the Institute's crown!"

The great Dr. Konig, Anat long ago realized, was a waddling sycophant, a bureaucratic parasite who had done no useful research in twenty years. Now that she had won the Leeuwenhoek Prize, he was afraid she might resign.

"Well, Dr. Konig, I'm thinking of leaving . . ."

Dr. Konig paled. "Why, Dr. Everett, this is all a surprise . . ."

". . . for the summer, that is. I need to rest and spend some time with my father."

Dr. Konig laughed, his face regaining its color. "Why, of course, Anat, dear. For the summer. You deserve it. The author of *Human Brain Vascular Development*"—he made a grand flourish with his arm—"is free to come and go as she pleases. We've always treated you well here, haven't we? But of course, you must miss your father. How is the amazing Hugh Everett and that marvelous house you grew up in? I'm still waiting for an invitation. Artists are such special people! I've always said that you were your father's daughter. The apple doesn't fall far . . ."

"Dr. Konig, if you'll excuse me just now. I have some odds and ends to do."

Konig walked up to her and smiled, wagging his finger. "Of course, Dr. Everett, I'll let you be. But please, stand up straight. Remember, tall women are the most beautiful!"

The train blew its whistle and began to move, startling Anat. A pale arm of steam waved past her window. Perhaps she had been too cruel to Konig, teasing him with her leaving. After all, he had always let her choose her work and methods. But the truth was it would all be over soon enough, though Konig did not know this. She looked at her watch, noticing her long, bony fingers. She sat up straight. Remember, tall women are the most beautiful! That, too, was her father's opinion, though he never applied it to Anat's gangling figure.

"Your mother was a goddess, tall and voluptuous," he would declare whenever Anat complained about her huge unfinished painting, *The Isotope of Love*, that stood in his cavernous domed studio. There the great El, father of the gods, his face her father's, swooped across the blood-red sky with "She That Marches upon the Sea," the laughing, lascivious Asherah, her pregnant mother, in his arms.

Anat imagined her naked mother posing on the blue chaise longue in the studio, head back, long throat exposed, belly swollen with Anat. Her mother's young flesh was painted an iridescent green, her father's sagging skin purple. And in certain corners of the canvas, beyond the soaring figures, were endless cellular processes, cuneiform-shaped organelles, and her father's favorite molecules, glucose, adenosine triphosphate, DNA. Her father was an obsessed man and had studied many things: neurophysiology ("Reality is the random coupling of a stimulus on the central nervous system!" he would say, quoting his idol, Schrödinger); ancient Ugaritic myths (hence her name, Anat, daughter of El and sister of Baal—"When you were born I was deep in study, I even corresponded with Virolleaud, the Columbus of the Ugarit tongue! I helped him translate the consonants *k'n'h'*—jealousy!"); astronomy; microscopic marine flora; the double helix; cramming them all, a great mishmash, into his paintings, sometimes hiding them in his famous medical illustrations for magazines.

"Well, at least I won't have to look at that every day," she told him when she left home for college. "And believe me, I doubt she looks like a goddess anymore."

"We've been through this before, Anat. Resentments cause

disease. Your mother, the great art lover, left solely on aesthetic principles; she thought she could inspire better. Foolish under the circumstances, I agree, but nothing personal. I don't begrudge bad judgment, just bad taste. And I've always tried to teach you, a painting is a painting. It's not your mother or anyone else. Besides, I'm grateful to her. She let me keep you. You were her present to me."

"A present to you!" Anat shrieked, stomping her skinny feet. "Are you crazy? A *present!*" And aesthetic principles? Her mother's *principles,* Anat suspected, had consisted solely of the fact that her husband was twenty years her senior and, during their year of marriage when Anat was born, he had grown heavier and more obtuse.

"Tickets! Tickets!" The bald conductor, clicking his hole puncher, passed down the aisle. Anat watched his hand, the sturdy network of bone and nerve, the ruddy insulation of skin, reach for her fare.

The Isotope of Love was almost forty years old now, a half-year older than Anat, and still unfinished. She should have destroyed it a long time ago. Maybe now she would. Her final act of liberation before disappearing into Chaos. First, she would send the annoying George Hanley, her father's new housekeeper, on some errand: "Don't worry so much, Mr. Hanley, I'll look in after my father. Please pick up my medicine. I've run out." She couldn't stand George Hanley, though she hadn't actually met him. "Who is he?" she asked her father when he told her he had hired a man.

"A bankrupt farmer from the county, a workaday apostle. My art, he believes, reflects the glory of God. Only I 'don't know Him yet.' Anyway, *he* has good references and I could use some help around here. I have so much to do."

Later, when Anat won the Leeuwenhoek Prize, she had phoned her father. Hanley answered.

"Oh, Dr. Everett, if I may respectfully say so, I feel as if I know you from your father's work. You are, if I may say so, ubiquitous around here!"

"Thank you. May I speak with my father?"

"Oh, I'm sorry, Mr. Everett is sleeping."

"Excuse me, please have him come to the phone. I have something important to tell him."

"With all due respect, Dr. Everett," Hanley's voice became high and sibilant, "it doesn't seem right to me to wake an eighty-year-old man from his sleep. Is it really *so* important?"

"Just have him call me!" She slammed down the receiver.

"That little George Hanley is always babying me," her father complained when he called back, though she knew he was secretly pleased. He had always loved attention and fussing, which in these last years had ebbed away. Once there had been a steady stream of pilgrims to their house, admirers, students, hangers-on. The cover article in the *Sunday Magazine*, "A Mentor for Our World," at the height of his fame said that "Hugh Everett, through his splendid scientific illustrations, reaffirms the essential role of the artist as teacher and enlightened humanist."

"I've become some sort of guru!" her father would groan, peeking into her bedroom, but then he hurried out to expand on one of his theories or answer the usual questions of unexpected visitors.

Anat would stay in her room and study the diatom collection her father had given her. "'Start small!' That's the advice Van Heurck, the renowned diatomist, gave me when I visited him in Antwerp. It's good advice, Anat. I've always held to it. We are, after all, predicated on the infinitesimal particles of life!"

Anat, gazing through her microscope at the stars, pinwheels, and chandelier shapes, heard her father's booming voice answer through the walls.

Why a round domed house?

"Squares and rectangles are harsh. They hound us into unnatural thinking. They cut off our breathing."

Do you really believe science and the humanities are the same?

"Science and the humanities are one! The verbal divisions are artificial!"

Oh, but what about God, Mr. Everett? Do you really deny Him?

"I have never found it helpful to invoke God in thinking about anything."

When will you finish The Isotope of Love?

"Some works are never finished! That is their essence."

Yes, after arriving at the house Anat would send Hanley on her errand. She would summon all her dwindling strength and crawl up the spiral stairway, "the double helix," into her father's studio while he was napping. The first flames would lick at the ebony hooves of El, then spread to the luxuriant green breasts of Asherah. She would also set fire to the blue chaise longue. Flames would fill the dome, with its clutter of paintings and paint, plaster casts, and epoxy bas-reliefs, then fly down into all the partitioned rooms of the house, swirling against the tall glass panes. Boom! The heat would blow out the windows.

When Anat was a little girl she had looked out a window and seen a convertible arrive. Recognizing her mother from *The Isotope of Love*, she ran panting, delirious with joy, across the house as her father's voice echoed above in the dome, "Anat, Anat! Your mother's here, come quickly!"

"Hello! Hello! Anyone home?" A tall woman entered the house, filling it with a sweet fragrance. Anat ran toward her mother, who, crouching, caught her and held her at arm's length. Anat gaped at her beauty, sky blue eyes and full black hair, which brushed against her bare shoulders. Though Anat understood from her father that color was only a device, "an energy frequency within the perceptual range of our nervous systems, an illusion," it surprised her that her mother's skin was white and smooth, not green. Until then she loved her mother though she knew her only from *The Isotope of Love*. Anat had been wearing paint-stained coveralls. "I'm helping Papa. I'm going to be an artist, too."

Her mother, looking Anat up and down, smiled weakly, finally giving her a little kiss on the forehead. "Of course you are."

"There really may be some modicum of talent there," her father said, the only time Anat heard him sound doubtful.

Her mother looked up at him and laughed. "Such a funny creature." She stood, and Anat realized she was taller than her former husband.

"Well, I should be going now, Hugh." She patted him on his grizzled cheek. "I just had a minute. I'm very happy with Jack, if you care to know. He's really going places. That abstract the Met just acquired, it's me. We're going to live in Italy—the climate is more suitable for artists. But really, Hugh, you and the kid will rot here in the sticks." She turned to Anat. "Oh, well, I guess I'm not the mommy type. Believe me, you're better off without me."

The week after Anat won the Leeuwenhoek and her name was in every newspaper in the world, she received a postcard from Italy. On the front was a painting of Andromeda.

Dear Darling,

Can't stop reading about you everywhere! I always knew you would be something one day! Jack's and my best to your dear father.

Brava! Brava!

Andrea

(your mother)

When she joined the Institute, Anat went to the Metropolitan and talked her way into the acquisitions storage area. The curator rolled his eyes and pulled a large, almost blank canvas from a vertical shelf, *Andrea's World #1*. Her mother, it appeared, was the only other color on the canvas, a thin green diagonal line.

The train crept several miles in tunnels beneath the city, then lurched into sunlight. Anat felt her heart tip over like a bag of groceries. For a moment she was dizzy. She thought how one day soon, with her heart so weakened, the whole balloon of her brain would collapse, deflated of oxygen and blood. Her eyes would pop open one last time and grasp the imprint of the world, her dying retinas like two photographic plates. Everything would stop.

By the time she reached the house, she would be exhausted. On her infrequent visits home, having lived so long with the right angles of the city, she had to adjust to the curves of the round house, her pie-piece bedroom, the steep spiral stairway to her father's domed studio, the half-moon of the living room.

Her father was proud of this house that appeared on the final twist of a long tree-lined drive. *"Domus ex nihilo!"* he'd proclaim whenever they returned from a local errand. The white, dome-topped cylinder, with its radial plantings of forsythia and boxwood, he had designed to resemble the delicate sunburst crown, the flaming corona radiata of a mature ovum. One summer they went up in a balloon, floating high above the rolling, green hills of the countryside. Her father pointed below to the small white bubble of their house and its spidery shrubbery.

"The pulsing ovum, the flashing nova, the coruscating latticework of crystal are all variations on a theme!" he shouted to Anat above the roar of the hot-air furnace. "They start from within and yearn outward! They defy Chaos!"

The train now traveled near the river's edge. Upstream, tiny white sails floated on the green water.

"We are predicated on the infinitesimal particles of life," her father had said. On the way back from receiving the

Leeuwenhoek in Zurich, she had caught a severe cold, and slowly, silently, the virus spread to her heart. One night, several weeks after her return, she dreamed that her heart was a big bloody sac, which she had to drag from place to place. When she awoke she realized her chest was full and tight. Her slender feet were puffy. Long ago her father had painted a pictorial essay for *Life*, "The Body Besieged." In one illustration, fantastic viruses, like flowery plankton and star-shaped diatoms, landed on a glistening heart, inserted their tentacles into the bright and spindly cardiac cells, and took over the blue nuclei, shattering them into infinite new baby creatures like themselves.

"What I'm feeling reminds me of that, remember!" she had told her father over the phone. "And I've never even been interested in the heart. It's one organ that bores me."

"That's ridiculous! There's nothing wrong with you. You're only thirty-nine. Are you drinking enough water?"

"Papa, you must accept my mortality!"

"Mortality? Nonsense! You are only nervous, frightened. Great accomplishment is a terrifying precipice! Come home and rest. All you ever do is work! I haven't seen you in months. My eyesight is failing, you know. It's difficult for me but I must press on. I have so much to do."

"Why must the conversation always turn back to you?"

"Well, if you think you're dying, come home. George Hanley will pick you up at the station. You, for one, will recognize him, he looks like a fetus. Anyway, everyone should die at home even if they never liked it. Have you seen a doctor?"

"Yes."

She had had every test: echo- and electrocardiograms, even a new magnetic resonance scan where she saw the chambers of her heart wink and pout.

"There is some damage, but minimal! With a little care, rest, and medication, you can lead a normal life," the doctor assured her, but she remained unconvinced. She knew otherwise.

"Our minds and bodies prophesy to each other," she mysteriously told one magazine interviewer.

"Our bodies and minds prophesy?" the interviewer, an arrogant young man, repeated, scribbling on his pad. He pressed on. "And what have you learned from all your work, Dr. Everett? I mean philosophically. That's what our readers would like to know. Has studying the developing brain made you understand yourself better? Has it made you understand the fundamental question, What is a person?"

"What is a person?" In her father's illustration for *Life* magazine, *The Watery Matrix*, her mother rose like Venus from the saline solvent of the sea. Next to her, enveloping her like a cloud, a pale green soul, a watery doppelgänger, mimicked her beauty. And swimming in the bottom of the primordial sea were strange aquatic creatures, one of which, with its pointed snout and thin lips, looked suspiciously like Anat, though its eyes were on top of its head, like a flat, floor-sweeping fish. Anat, then in high school, ran up to the studio and threw the magazine at her father. It glanced off *The Isotope of Love*.

"Papa! You promised to leave me out of your awful artwork! When did I ever pose for that?"

Her father sat at an easel, his heavy shoulders sagging. "You didn't. I've internalized your entire being."

"And where exactly is there room?"

"In the confines of my heart," he said, forming that sad organ with his hands.

Anat looked up. The interviewer was staring at his watch, waiting for her answer. "Well, Dr. Everett, have you had enough time to think about the question? Shall we continue?"

"Yes. No. I have another appointment."

Her father had called her at the Institute. "That was some terse interview in *Time*. That's my daughter, only smarter than me. Our molecules must be on the same frequency. I never liked giving interviews myself. You know my new theory that some memories are passed down in the resonant frequencies of molecules, a whole new undiscovered code . . ."

"The difference between us, Papa, is that you speculate, I investigate, and I'm really busy now." She was working on a new project, the fluid compartments of the brain, the ventricles, cisterns, and their continuum, the intercellular spaces. She was entering Konig's abandoned territory, continuing where his genius fell short. She had just sectioned the primordial nervous system of a human embryo onto slides. Time was critical. Her hands moved rapidly among the fixatives and dyes. Though she was still quick, her old fascination was gone. Often before, when working on her atlas, Anat would imagine her own brain rising in an amnion sea, unfurling like a fern, blooming into arteries and veins, axons and dendrites, ripening into lobes and hemispheres and memories. Such thoughts filled her with delight. "As if I myself were present at Creation!" she told Konig when she joined the Institute.

"Why, that's a very charming thought, my dear, beautifully expressed," he said, patting her hand, "truly lovely and charming!" They were sitting on massive leather chairs in his wood-paneled office. He handed her a bowl of sour balls. "Care for any?" She smiled and reached for one even though she hated candy. In those days she was foolish enough to worship Konig for his pathbreaking work on the ventricles of the brain. She felt so lucky to be working under him. "He is the new Galen, the new Vesalius!" everyone said. "Heaven knows what he will do next! He'll be the first to win a second Leeuwenhoek!" But all Konig did in the twelve years she knew him was waddle through the corridors of the Institute or travel to international meetings, rehashing the same papers over and over, and fawn over scientists and donors and government representatives. In the first months after winning her own Leeuwenhoek, Anat had thought she must rededicate herself to her work, to recover her former delight.

Dr. Konig was now peeking into the laboratory while she was still on the phone with her father. He smiled and waved like a child. "Perhaps, Dr. Everett, you will win a second Leeuwenhoek!" She glared at him, then turned away. She held the phone to her cheek with her shoulder, picking up a slide tray with her hands.

"Now I'm really busy, Papa. Everyone's interrupting me. Why are you calling?"

"I'm just feeling under the weather, as they say. At my age any change in the atmosphere will do it. It doesn't take much to throw our tenuous fluid nature out of whack. We are, after all, liquid creatures: condensed from the clouds, bubbled up from the seas—"

"Damn!" The tray of slides had slipped from her hands, shattering on the floor. Three weeks' work wasted. Anat felt exhausted. She looked at her skinny hands in disgust.

The shiny river reminded Anat of faraway places she had never been to and now would never visit. She had always been too involved in her research to travel. Even on evenings and weekends, she found herself in the laboratory peering through her microscope, charting the blood vessels that flowed in embryological time, coursing from one part of the brain to the next, through gray matter and white, through nuclei and tracts, relinquishing some pathways, annexing others. Now looking out the train window she imagined tropical shores with breezy palms and colorful bougainvillea instead of evergreens and birch and maple. But she had, of course, seen greater things. In Zurich, at the presentation ceremony for the Leeuwenhoek Prize, Dr. Fontaine, the head of the Academy, said, "Dr. Anat Everett has seen what others have failed to see and now has shared with us her vision. She has taught us to see!"

A woman with a baby entered the coach and sat across the aisle from Anat. The baby, sitting in its mother's arms, fixed two dark eyes on Anat, carrying her image to its brain. Once in a three-page foldout for *The Mercury*, "The Seeing Eye," a child Anat swam in a distant green pond and simultaneously, inverted through the prism of the human lens, across a pink and buoyant retinal sky and yet again, transmitted through the magic lantern of the optic nerves, across the white hills of visual cortex. She had not noticed that her father had drawn her naked and she'd brought the magazine to show-and-tell. A boy in her elementary class held up the picture. "Look! Everyone can see Anat's flat titties and her secret place." And the other children giggled, "Titties, titties, titties . . ." She had the presence of mind to say, "At least I'm famous," but she screamed at her father when she got home. "I don't want to be in any of your stupid pictures! Everyone makes fun of me!"

"No one is in any picture. You are right where you are," he insisted, though she soon found herself not where she was but in a series of advertisements commissioned by a pharmaceutical company: Anat breathing in the breath of a cloudborne Aeolus for an asthma medication advertisement, her lungs expanding through her translucent pediatric chest, her alveoli bunched, glistening like grapes; Anat in a blue pinafore, running through a bowel-like maze, just one step ahead of the pink, flowing river of bismuth sulfate; and Anat lying in a hospital bed, feverish, an intravenous tube in her arm. After that, when she posed, she would grimace, turn her foot this way and that, or twist her arms together. Her father would sit and frown and continue painting, scrutinizing her from time to time with dim fish eyes through thick aquarium-like lenses. Later they would have it out. "What's this fresh outburst? Am I asking too much of your time? Do you resent something? Do you feel abused, neglected? Don't you have enough toys and books and dresses?"

"Just forget it. I'm not posing anymore. Pretend you're blind and can't see me!"

"Yes, we were blind," Dr. Fontaine had said at the Leeuwenhoek ceremony, smiling gently at Anat on the dais. "But now Dr. Everett has shown us her vision of wonder and beauty." Then he went on, telling the audience how "alone, through painstaking work and consummate artistry, she deciphered the great and transient Primordial Cerebral Vein, revealing its mystery and the inevitability of its course." And how her "extraordinary camera lucida drawings, layered as they were like slices from the microtome, took one's breath away. She is, you know, the daughter of a famous artist!" Anat walked up to the podium in a violet dress with a silver belt, and matching silver high-heeled shoes that made her look even taller. The crowd rose for a standing ovation. "Ah, she is lovelier than ever, truly regal," Konig said later to all the scientific luminaries who gathered around at the reception. His face was smooth and pink, basking in the stolen glow of her genius. He took hold of her hand for a moment. "It's too bad your father isn't here, dear."

George Hanley was waiting for her on the station platform. Looking out the coach window, she knew him instantly. He was short and thin, his head small and smooth, almost microcephalic. She could not guess his age. She took in a deep breath. Sometimes she thought she could cut into her chest with a knife and carve out her heart like some spoiled and fleshy fruit.

"You're just as I imagined you, or shall I say how your father imagined you for me," George Hanley said, picking up her small bag. "It is most certainly a great honor for me to meet you. Yes, it most certainly is. You must be tired from your trip."

"Yes, Mr. Hanley, I am."

"They're beautiful, sunshiny, like you, if I may respectfully say so, Dr. Everett," Hanley said.

Guarding the long driveway to the country house, and partly hidden in the overgrown woods, were dozens of tall, bronze sunflowers, each with the face of the child Anat. She had so looked forward to them the day her father placed two straws up her nose and smeared her face and hair with Vaseline. She was seven. Her father then covered her head with plaster. Her heart beat in anticipation. "How long does bronze last?" she whispered, trying not to move, dimly aware of an undeserved immortality.

"Thousands and thousands of years. Now, stop talking and don't move. I'm trying to concentrate."

The plaster grew hot as it dried but Anat held still. Her father poured cold water over her head and cut the plaster mold off. That night, her hair still greasy despite a bath and shampoo, she climbed the spiral stairway to her father's studio and looked up at the stars through the glass oculus of the dome. No matter what her father claimed, she knew that God lived among the twinkling stars. Anat made a wish that her beautiful mother, the art lover, would come back to see the sculptures. She closed her eyes and God flowed through her like a warm breeze.

Anat cried the day the sunflowers came back from the foundry. "I'm so ugly!" Her bronze expression was grim, her nose long and sharp. A bubble in the mold made one eye look puckered, diseased. "Oh, Papa, my eye, my eye!" She ran to the bathroom mirror to see if it was so.

"There's nothing wrong with your eye!" her father said. "You're just like your mother. Repeat after me, 'I am not Art. Art I am not.'"

For weeks she wore sunglasses. Too much light might wear out her eyes. She looked through illustrations in *Grant's Anatomy*, slowly deciphering the strange and beautiful words. Several times a day she checked her eye in the mirror, pulling at the lid, looking for signs of disease. She peered at the soft brown iris, the black hole of the pupil, and scrutinized the gleamy white surface of sclera and the pink bulge of lacrimal gland beneath the corner of the upper lid.

Now, on the drive to the house, she saw that the bronze faces and their puckered eyes had taken on a patina from the years: green with flecks of gold and red. The bronze stems were covered with vines.

"They're like the blessed angels that hover around us whom we are not fit to see," George Hanley said, his breath smelling like peppermint, "the little angels that coax the grass to grow."

Anat, tired, sighed.

Hanley suddenly stopped the car. "With all due respect, Dr. Everett, I know you're very brilliant and famous, but how else do these things happen? How do the trees and grasses and even people grow? Do you think it all happens by itself in a laboratory? He was breathing hard and sweating in his flesh-colored rayon suit. Anat realized he was also wearing a hat and tie despite the heat.

"Mr. Hanley, I'm not arguing with you. I didn't even say anything. It's hot. I'm not well."

"Even your father's work is inspired by God."

Anat looked down at her thin hands. They seemed like alien creatures, beings apart. She willed them to open and shut. She looked up at Hanley. "I'd like to hear you tell the old atheist that."

Hanley drew in his breath, his little chest puffing up. "Oh, I always do, and he hears me. I speak my mind. Respectfully, Dr. Everett, but I speak it. I'm not one who's afraid to speak his mind. Why, I've told Mr. Everett, why waste time on those silly myths the Ubanits made up."

"*Ugarits*, Mr. Hanley."

"Ugarits . . . whatever. Now the Bible, I told him, that's different, it's all true. And he listens."

"Oh, really, he does?"

"Really, Dr. Everett."

They rode silently the last hundred meters to the house.

George Hanley began climbing up the spiral stairway to the studio. "Mr. Everett! Mr. Everett, we've returned!"

Anat waited below in the half-moon of the living room.

"Dr. Everett! Oh, my God, Dr. Everett!" George Hanley's shrill voice reverberated above in the dome. "Oh, my God! Your father! Come quick!"

Anat hurried halfway up the staircase but, weak and dizzy,

stopped and closed her eyes. Holding onto the banister, she imagined Death floating down the oculus, taking her father by surprise. "Why, Mr. Hugh Everett"—Death was the flattering Dr. Konig—"you can't imagine how your life's work has influenced me! It's so nice to be here. Please, come this way. I must show you something. As for your daughter. So tall and beautiful! You must be proud. I'm so glad she's coming, too."

"Oh, my God, Dr. Everett!" George Hanley came down the stairway and helped Anat up the last steps. "Please, Dr. Everett! You must be strong!"

"Wait a moment. I can't." She had to sit on the stairhead. She felt for her wrist, seeking a pulse. It was faint, thready.

"Please, Dr. Everett!"

Anat looked straight up at the cloudless blue sky through the oculus and then across the smooth white hemisphere. Her father was slumped on the blue chaise longue. His palette and brushes lay scattered nearby on the floor.

George Hanley moved away from Anat and stood back before the chaise, pulling at his face with his little hands. "Oh, my God, I can't believe this happened while I was out! I always said this is no place for an old man to sleep. It's simply too hot. He should take his naps in a normal bed. But your father wouldn't listen to me. Oh, Dr. Everett! Oh, dear God."

Suddenly she heard her father's voice.

"What is it, Hanley! Be still! I'm not dead yet!" Her father was rising from the chaise, fumbling with his thick glasses. He put them on and saw his daughter. "Anat, Hanley always thinks I'm dead."

"Oh, Papa." Her voice was a whisper. A cool breeze moved up the stairwell. She tried to stand. She was now less dizzy but still had to lean against the banister.

"I fell asleep working." He nodded to the opposite end of the room.

Anat slowly turned and looked to where *The Isotope of Love* had always stood. There, where El and Asherah once flew, lay a blue sleeping Adam, her father in his youth, in the tall grass of a twilight Eden. And she, Anat, Mother Eve, hovered above him. Tall, supple as life. En pointe. Condensing into milky flesh, woven from a whirling net of arteries and crystalline ribs that spiraled up through her. Her hair was long and wild, tangled with brilliant molecules. She appeared bewildered, looking out at the world for the first time.

"I'm so sorry, Mr. Everett, but I thought . . ." George Hanley cried.

Her father, ignoring him, walked over to Anat and took her by the arm.

"So? Are you really not well?" Though he was old and stout, her father moved vigorously. His hold was firm and close. He led her to the painting.

"Oh, Papa."

Anat let herself be carried along.

At that moment she felt buoyant, weightless, her life flowing toward her full of marvel and mystery, a swift stream of wonder through Chaos.

Chagall

THE LITTLE POET

✤   ✤   ✤

"*Le soleil! Le soleil!*"

Toby Sahl skipped down the steps of the Jerusalem Sheraton and greeted the sunlight. His parents anxiously followed
his narrow figure from the terrace while they finished breakfast. He glanced up sideways and for an instant saw, at the
bowl rim of vision, the sun's fiery waves and brilliant storms
of light. He had better hurry now, he thought, because there
was only half an hour to look around, as today was set aside
for visiting. He turned and ran along Agron Street, scaling
the stone apartment buildings and towering cypress with his
eyes, breathing a sweet fragrance from Paradise. He tried to
transform the charm, the feel, "the insistent wonder of the

moment," as he once read, into a poem. When it was done he would send it to the Young Ontario Poets' Competition.

Over these pink hills
I am the wind
a glowing day star
a fragrance on air . . .

Toby thought it would sound even better in French, but he'd only just finished the fifth grade back home in Windsor and he was still learning the language and anyway the competition was in English. He needed six poems to complete his entry. Last year he was runner-up, his work "showing great promise and sophistication." This year he would use his summer trip to inspiring advantage. And though he never really saw her, he knew his muse hovered above like an angel, handing him the delicate threads that he spun into gold.

He would rather have gone to France, at least for a stopover, because that was where great poets and writers went. Still, he was excited to be in a foreign country. And one day he would go to France, by then speaking French fluently. He would board the airplane and say complicated things to the astonished stewardesses: "Are you familiar with the collection in the Louvre? I so look forward to its enchantments!" He already knew English and Hebrew, and if you knew two languages, it was easier to learn a third and then a fourth and then a fifth and so on. Every evening he sat with his father, studying the Bible and commentaries. But those ancient sounds, now that he had discovered French, seemed dark and flat, like endless cups of cold tea. It was often tiresome having a rabbi for a father, someone who did not appreciate the beautiful poetry he was constantly reading. "God's words are poetry, too," his father would say heavily, his tall figure leaning toward him. But words, Toby thought, running down Agron Street, waving his skinny arms like a bird, should be light and flashing and airborne.

Sometimes he would go to the public library to borrow French poetry books even though he could not understand them. He loved the titles, *Les Fleurs du Mal* or *Hymne à la Beauté*. He felt the tickle of the words way back in his throat and just beneath his skin. One day he would write an epic poem in French and be made Chevalier de France.

"Close your eyes! Imagine Paris!" he urged his parents several weeks before at the Sabbath evening meal. They had just sung "In Jerusalem" and were talking about their forthcoming trip.

His mother, twisting a lock of brown hair behind her ear, glanced nervously at his father. "We really don't know anyone there and we don't speak the language. If we were Montrealers, it would be different."

His father, tapping a long finger on the tablecloth, agreed. "French and France are very nice, Toby, but you still have to improve your Hebrew. It's the language of your ancestors. And we're going to the Land of Miracles. You'll like that."

"Oh, *mes parents!*" Toby jumped up on his chair and stood, arms outstretched, as upon a mountaintop. "Moses spoke seventy languages! French and Italian and Indian and Spanish and German and Chinese and Swahili and Japanese and Mexican and Swedish and Albanian and Portuguese—"

"Dear, please sit down, you'll fall!" his mother said. And

later he overheard his father say crossly to his mother, "Where does this all come from?"

Now, running on Agron Street, Toby looked straight up to the sky. He imagined each step carried him a vast distance, as with Jacob, for whom, his father once told him, distances were miraculously shortened. Toby stretched out one thin leg and traveled thirty kilometers. There were so many weird miracles in the Bible. He thought he should write a poem about them. Even now one grew rapidly in his head like Jonah's gourd.

> The stars bowed and scraped
> The Moon complained
> and grew small
> The rock, smitten
> bled . . .

How strange, too, he thought, to be suddenly standing on the other side of this rocklike planet in a fragrant city. There was no fragrance in Windsor except the sour smell of mash that filled the air from the distillery. Compared with the great Earth, *and the fullness thereof,* Toby Sahl was less than a dot, a minuscule speck, an atom, now expanding to cover the globe with the radiant ink of poetry. A cloud moved overhead, veiling the sun, but Toby continued to skip across the hills like a ram.

> A molecule, a cell
> a drop in the ocean
> all becomes one
> the world contracts
> sunlit . . .

Suddenly he tripped and fell, tearing his pants and scraping his knee.

Later, in the hotel room, his father said he must be more careful. "Keep your eyes on the pavement." Toby sat on the side of the bed while his mother painted his knee with iodine.

"*Ma mère*, are the germs here different from back home? Will I get a fatal infection?"

"God forbid!"

Toby saw the sad procession following his coffin: his weeping parents supporting each other, his schoolmates, his teachers, everyone crying so. Yes, he must do something. It was all too sad even for words. He must—he must defy Death!

Suddenly he jumped up, knocking the iodine bottle out of his mother's hand, splattering the sheets. He clutched his head between his hands and quoted Donne in a high voice.

"Death be not proud, though some have called thee
 Mighty and dreadful, for, thou art not soe!"

His mother had been happy that morning. Before breakfast she had combed her thin brown hair for a long time and even put on lipstick and eye shadow. They were going to visit Julia Glass, whom she hadn't seen in twenty years. Toby's mother and Julia grew up together in Winnipeg, and Julia married David Leon. "They were romantics and pioneers," Toby's mother said dreamily. "They just picked up and followed their hearts. Julia was a great beauty. She was my best friend. Funny, you never forget your best friend even if you're half a world away and out of touch. Their little girl is two years younger than you, Toby. I remember because a letter came from Julia right after we moved to Windsor and that was when you were two years old."

In the taxi Toby began reciting Herrick loudly.

"Whenas in silks my Julia goes,
  Then, then, methinks, how sweetly flows
  That liquefaction of her clothes."

"You're missing the scenery, Toby," his father said.

"*Enchanté, Madame et Monsieur,*" Toby said, rushing into the Leons' apartment ahead of his parents. He looked around the high-ceilinged living room and then back at the Leons. Mr. Leon was short and stocky and ugly, but Mrs. Leon was tall with dark eyes and light blond hair. "You're more beautiful than the legend."

"Why, thank you. He's quite a gentleman." Mrs. Leon smiled as she embraced his mother. Mrs. Leon's teeth were very white and perfect. She held Toby's mother at arm's length. "I can't believe you're finally here. You look wonderful!"

"Oh, so do you, Julia!"

"Let me hug you again. We were so worried when we heard about your surgery. Thank God you're all right."

"Thank God," Mr. Leon said.

"Yes, thank God," Mrs. Sahl said. "The surgeon said he got everything. So the Rabbi and I decided it was time to go on the trip we always wanted."

Julia took Toby's mother's hand. "I'm so happy you did. Well, here comes our Yaffa."

A heavy little girl with black pigtails ran panting into the room. Discovering the company, she stopped suddenly in her tracks. Her face was pink and sweaty.

"Everyone, say hello to our Yaffa," Mr. Leon said, extending his arm to his daughter.

"Yaffa. Charm!" Toby translated.

The girl glared at him.

Toby's father corrected him. "*Yaffa* means 'beauty.'"

"*Enchanté, Mademoiselle.*"

Mrs. Leon put her hand gently on the girl's shoulder. "Yaffa, Toby is from Canada just like your father and me, and he knows French."

Yaffa shook off her mother's hand and walked up to Toby. She stared into his eyes, "Canada, caca." Her rough accent made Toby think of an old woman.

"Really, Yaffa!" Mrs. Leon smiled and shrugged her shoulders at the guests. "Yaffa really doesn't know much about Canada. She was born here."

Toby knew there was something cruel and tragic and therefore poetic in Yaffa's weirdness that made her mean. Though Yaffa was fat, he knew her really to be small and bruised and lonely and despised. "Don't judge people," his father always said, "until you are in their shoes." Toby took out a little notebook from his shirt pocket and wrote,

Beauty unfolds
in sad swollen hearts
Away! Away!
Away, pathetic loneliness!

"How is the construction business?" Toby's father asked Mr. Leon with interest.

"I'm glad you asked." Mr. Leon's voice boomed. "Business is great! I'm building a new hotel on the Dead Sea. We'll take you out there. And I'm on the city council, so I'm always very busy. That old mayor doesn't work half as hard as I do." Mr. Leon had dark hair like his daughter. Toby found it difficult to look at him because of the long hairs growing out of his ears. "Now people are starting to say, 'David, why don't you run for mayor? You're the man who's got what it takes!'"

Mr. Leon showed them a collection of prints, framed in glass boxes, hanging on the living room walls. "It's my hobby. Incunabula. Do you know what that means, Toby?" Mr. Leon put a thick hand on the boy's neck. "The frames are hermetically sealed. By definition the pages were printed before A.D. 1500. I've been collecting them for years. It's also a good investment. This one is from the famous poet Ibn Gabirol."

"Toby writes poetry, too," his mother said. "Last year he was runner-up in the Young Ontario Poetry Contest."

"Poets' Competition, *ma mère.*"

"My sister Belle wrote poetry and would have been famous if she hadn't died so young," Mr. Leon said. "But anyway, everything worthwhile has already been written."

"'Nothing is new under the sun!'" Toby quoted, looking into the next room.

"Look, *mes parents,* they have a baby grand!"

"We bought it to encourage Yaffa but she never practices," Mrs. Leon said.

"You know, Julia, I still can't get over how young you look. You haven't aged a bit since high school," Mrs. Sahl said.

"Well, I think you haven't changed either."

"But just look at my gray hair!"

Toby went into the other room and began playing Debussy's first *Arabesque* with lots of pedal. Yaffa ran out of the apartment, slamming the front door.

"She's sure full of pep," Mrs. Sahl said.

Mr. Leon walked over to the piano in the next room and slowly began closing the keyboard lid. "By the way, isn't Toby a girl's name?"

Toby got his fingers out just in time. "It's a boy's name, too."

"And you write poetry?"

Toby showed Mr. Leon a page from his notebook. "I just wrote this." Mr. Leon glanced at it and handed it back. "Write something I would like."

As the Sahls were leaving, Julia Leon said, "Remember, Saturday lunch."

Toby and his parents woke up early on Saturday so they could walk to the Wall for morning services and still be in time for lunch at the Leons'. They entered the Old City through Jaffa Gate. Its heavy arches reminded Toby of Yaffa's grossness.

So sad and wretched
at Jaffa Gate
her pitiful eyes
like two Bethlehem stars . . .

He would have liked to write this inspiration in his note-book so he wouldn't forget, but he wasn't allowed to write on the Sabbath.

They walked through the narrow streets of the souk. The unfamiliarly spicy smells made Toby feel nauseated. He almost walked into a side of beef hanging in an open butcher shop. He bent over feeling he had to vomit but nothing came up. He then closed his eyes and held his nose as his parents, each with a hand on either shoulder, steered him through the crowded streets.

"Okay, you can look now," his mother said as they came out into a vast, sunny plaza.

In the distance the great stone Wall was bright and golden in the morning light. His father's eyes filled with tears as they approached. His hand still held Toby's shoulder. "The Wall is thousands of years old and was part of the Temple. I've always dreamed of seeing it. The Wall is heavy with history."

As they approached, Toby broke away and ran leaping toward the men's section of the Wall. *"Le mur! Le mur!"* When he reached it he turned around and, leaning over, pretended to hold it up like Atlas. "Whew! It is heavy! I'm breaking my back!"

His father ran and caught him, grabbing him by the neck.

"Please, stop it. Not here!"

Toby sank to the ground, flailing his arms and legs. People started gathering around.

"Toby! I said to stop!"

The boy suddenly got up and brushed himself off. "You might have pressed on my spinal cord or something and accidentally killed me!"

"My God, Toby, you're eleven years old. Act your age."

"On our next big trip we're going to France, probably by ship. We had to get this trip out of the way for religious purposes," Toby was telling Yaffa as she silently loaded an enormous pile of fried potatoes onto her plate. Mrs. Leon also served chicken, which Yaffa wouldn't touch. "In France we'll tour Paris and the Louvre and the Île de France, which is like an island of land, *surrounded by land,* and Brittany and Normandy . . ."

"Yaffa is a vegetarian," Mrs. Leon explained to Toby's parents. "She's very sensitive. She's opposed to taking the life of animals. Remember Vera Levi in high school? She was a vegetarian, wasn't she?"

". . . and Champagne, which is where they get the name from, and the Riviera on La Mer Méditerranée . . ."

"When she was only five years old, she said to my husband, 'Where does steak come from?'"

"Yes, she said 'steaky.'" Mr. Leon looked at his daughter and smiled. "When we finally told her, she started screaming and hitting her mother!" While he was talking a fleck of chicken stuck to his bottom lip. "What a little genius!"

". . . and Toulouse, which is somewhere in the middle. Did you ever hear of Toulouse-Lautrec? And the Auvergne . . . ?"

"Does she get enough protein?" Toby's mother asked. "Toby hardly eats anything, which is why he's so small. I think he lives on air. But you really can't force children to eat. They say they each have their own inner balance point somewhere in the brain, and that—"

Yaffa suddenly started banging the table with her fists in rhythm and shouting a hymn in a high, shrill voice:

"*Menucha v'simcha*
Rest and joy
A light to Your people
The Sabbath Day."

Mr. Leon joined her, singing in harmony:

"A day of delights
The Sabbath Day
Rest and joy
A light to Your people."

Toby's parents didn't know this tune but tried to hum along. Toby couldn't finish his train of thought because of the commotion. At home, at least, his parents sang softly.

"That was beautiful, Yaffa." Mr. Leon leaned over and patted her on the head. He turned to Toby's parents. "Yaffa doesn't like to talk much but she loves to sing. She gets it from my family."

"That's true. There were several prominent cantors in David's family," Mrs. Leon said. "Remember Cantor Haleri in Winnipeg? He was David's cousin."

"Well, everybody, don't stop eating on account of the music!" Mr. Leon said.

"I can't imagine what they must go through with her. I'm heartsick," Toby's mother was saying to his father as they walked back to the hotel. "Poor Julia! I don't know how she's able to handle that child." Toby was following behind them, looking up at the sky, trying to remember what he had thought of the first morning. He had forgotten to write it down.

> O hills . . .
> . . . fragrant hills
> the wind . . .
> O fragrance . . .

He couldn't remember. He almost tripped again but his father caught him. "Toby! Eyes on the pavement!" Tonight, Toby thought, he would be sure to leave his notepad under his pillow. Perhaps his muse would come to him in his sleep. He knew that every great artist had a muse, an angel, a goddess of inspiration, and he must have one, too, even though he could not see her. He made a wish that tonight she would appear.

"Look, there's the president's house." His father pointed to a sprawling building that looked like a series of boxes.

Toby looked up. *"Maison de Monsieur Président!"*

The next day, Mr. Leon drove up in front of the Jerusalem Sheraton. "This is my new Peugeot. French cars are very popular here." Mr. Leon asked Toby's father to sit up front. Toby and his mother joined Yaffa and Julia in the backseat. "The kids can each sit near a window so they won't be bored," Mr. Leon said.

"Peugeot, Peugeot, Peugeot," Toby whispered to himself, again wishing they had gone to France.

"We almost had to cancel today because Toby had stomach problems, but this new liquid medicine really worked for him." His mother showed Mrs. Leon the bottle. "I brought it along just in case."

"Yes, I've heard about it. But we never get sick. We're fortunate that way."

Yaffa held her nose and made loud farting noises with her lips.

"Yaffa, you promised," her mother said, and then she smiled at Toby's mother. They drove south out of the city and soon were on a high barren hill overlooking the wide desert. In the distance lay the long opal haze of the Dead Sea.

"It's the lowest place on earth"—Mr. Leon slowed the car so they could enjoy the view—"which gives it great healthful properties."

"*La Mer Morte!*" Toby interrupted triumphantly, and he wrote the phrase in his notebook. He then whispered to himself, *"La Mer Morte, La Mer Morte, La Mer Morte."*

Yaffa began squirming in her seat, playing with the lock button on her door and rolling her window up and down.

"Yaffa, there's not much room for moving about," Mrs. Leon said. "And the air-conditioning is on."

"This is all so beautiful," Toby's mother said. Her eyes filled with tears. "I can't believe I'm seeing you again. I thought I'd never make this trip. And now we're together, halfway around the world from our childhood on old Victoria Avenue in Winnipeg!"

Julia gently patted her on the hand. "Time passes like a dream."

The car was now on the edge of a great escarpment. Mr. Leon stopped the car. "This is part of the Great Rift Valley that extends all the way from East Africa!"

Toby opened his eyes as wide as he could to absorb the experience and then started writing in his notebook.

Time
Time and Space
Here and there
a sea of salt
and tears . . .

"My new hotel is bound to be a great success," Mr. Leon continued as he drove on. "The other hotels here are always booked. It's time for a new one. The Dead Sea is rich, in minerals, potassium, phosphate, bromine, and it's a tonic for bathers. Toby, did you know we all contain minerals? Poets should know facts. My sister Belle always told me that and Yaffa knows it, too. Yaffa is the spitting image of her. Anyway, there are two layers of water in the Dead Sea that don't really mix. The deeper layer is the saltier and more ancient."

"David is quite an expert," Toby's mother said to Julia.

"Yes, if something interests him, he learns all about it and becomes an authority. It's amazing."

"Are they still mining the Dead Sea?" Toby's father asked thoughtfully.

"There are enough minerals to last another thousand years."

Toby added to his poem.

Yea, a thousand years
of salt . . .

He thought his poem was quite good. And he had read that
poetry need not explain the world, but rather, suggest it.

His mother peeked over into his notepad. "Why, that's very
nice, Toby." He decided to read it out loud to get a general reaction, even though he wasn't yet sure of the title. He felt a
slow and loud delivery would work best.

"Time
Time and Space—"

Mr. Leon interrupted him, speaking loudly. "There are
bacteria that live in the Dead Sea that may cause a scientific
revolution. They were just discovered by a scientist. Did you
know that, Toby?" Toby didn't, and had to begin his poem again.

"Time
Time and Space
Here and there—"

The road was now steep and winding. Mr. Leon drove with
many abrupt starts and stops. "Anyway, my hotel will be a
great success. By the time you're all here on your next vacation,
you'll be able to stay with us there. Won't that be convenient
and fun, Toby?"

Toby was having trouble reading his poem with all the talking and motion. He started to feel carsick but he persisted.

"A seal of salt
and tears!"

Mr. Leon made an abrupt turn to avoid a rock that had fallen onto the road. Toby was squeezed against his startled mother.

"Yea! A thousand years
of—"

Suddenly the door on Yaffa's side sprang open and the girl fell out of the moving car, disappearing over the embankment. "Yaffa! Yaffa!" Mrs. Leon screamed. Her husband slammed on the brakes. Toby's forehead struck the back of Mr. Leon's seat.

"Oh, my God! I found her! She's alive!" Mr. Leon yelled as his heavy figure scrambled over the embankment. Mrs. Leon and Toby's parents stood terrified, frozen next to the car like pillars. Toby felt light-headed and leaned against his mother. A moment later, Mr. Leon was carrying Yaffa back up to the road, his clothes all dusty. "It's a miracle!" he kept yelling. "All those bushes were there to catch her or else she would have fallen clear into the valley!" Yaffa's shoulder was dislocated; it bulged above her torn dress. And though she was streaked with blood, she only had a few cuts and scratches.

"It's a miracle!" Toby's mother finally said. "And she's not even crying!" Mr. Leon motioned for them all to get back into the car. "Yaffa never cries."

He put his daughter carefully on her mother's lap.

"Everything will be all right, darling," Mrs. Leon said. "Everything will be all right." Yaffa turned her head and glared at Toby.

"Internal injuries can fool you," Mr. Leon kept saying during the drive to the hospital in Jerusalem. "They're silent killers. Now everyone just be quiet; that's why we had this accident, because there was so much commotion in the car. It's impossible to drive when everyone's talking at one time." Mr. Leon looked at Toby in his rearview mirror.

Toby felt dizzy but the feeling passed. He fingered a large bump on the side of his forehead while his mother held him in her arms. "It's a miracle! It's a miracle!" she kept saying.

At the hospital a doctor came into the waiting room to tell them that Yaffa would be fine. "Her shoulder's back in place. She'll be her old self in no time." Toby's mother and Mrs. Leon burst into tears and hugged each other.

"Thank God we weren't going fast and that I have quick reflexes," Mr. Leon said, hugging his daughter as she came out of the examining room, her arm in a white sling.

Toby felt dizzy again. He saw his mother worriedly ask the doctor to look at him. "He's white as a sheet. He bumped his head hard in the car." The doctor had long black hair and was very beautiful. She looked at Toby's forehead and smiled. "Everything will be all right," she said kindly. Toby heard Mr. Leon's voice. "Oh, there's nothing wrong with him. He's jealous of the attention Yaffa's getting."

The doctor had Toby lie on a stretcher and then flashed a brilliant light in each eye. He felt a fluttering in his heart as the doctor seemed to fade away. Toby reached out for his notebook, which now floated up and hovered above him. He joyously saw the great muse, the dazzling goddess of poetry enter the room. *And she was great in beauty and well favored,* like the doc-

tor and Mrs. Leon and his mother. He felt her warm hand
guiding his as he wrote:

> My desert days
> Have seen such miracles
> Afloat in hazy pools
> of memory . . .

Then a letter from the Young Ontario Poets' Competition
came forth and bowed before him. The words and sentences
flew off the page in ribbons. *The competition was indeed fierce, but it
was the lines of "La Mer Morte" that won us over. They are otherworldly,
full of feeling and depth.* The letter went on and explained, with
sparkling words and sweet voices, the value of the prize to the
young poet, how it would ensure his fame, how crowds would
gather and applaud, how his poems would be translated into
French and Chinese and Hebrew and every language on earth.
And how the air we all breathed was forever altered, and how
the sun, rising higher every day, shone with a new light.

IF I HAVE FOUND FAVOR
IN YOUR EYES

"This world is a vestibule," I told my mother in the minimalist style that had evolved in communications with my parents. I was fourteen the year after my parents' unexplained divorce, and from within that silent void I had become suddenly infatuated, buoyant with newfound faith.

"What is that supposed to mean?" My mother was sitting at her piano, in front of a score. "I really don't have time for this." She turned back to the keyboard and resumed practicing. Before, while my parents were still married, she had championed my father's music, with its ecstatic rhythms and yearning melodies that rose from a boiling clamor like life out of the primordial seas. Now that they were divorced, she was playing more of the old warhorses again, "the tried and true, the guaranteed engagement pieces," as her manager and closest friend, Gloria, called them—Rachmaninoff's Third, Prokofiev's Second. And her career was accelerating. She was busier than ever. "Your mom's finally hitting her stride, Amir," Gloria had told me. "She's *there*."

It was a Saturday morning in winter, and my mother was preparing Strauss's *Burlesque for Piano and Orchestra* for a tour in the spring.

"I'm a single parent now and have to make a living. I can't just play Ivri's crap anymore," I recently had heard her telling Gloria. She had always called my father by his last name. More frequently, since the divorce, she began referring to him as "that little Israeli," although my father had lived in America since boyhood.

My mother had never given up her own name, Everett, which was really more like my father's name than she cared to acknowledge, for it was one of those names embraced by a previous generation, meant to cover tracks and obliterate traces, derived from Yivrayski, the Polish analogue of my father's Jew-designating label. As for me, I am the hyphenated, etymologically redundant Amir Everett-Ivri.

I stood there while she ignored me and ran through several measures. When she was concentrating on music she cocked her head to one side. Her long black hair, which was now starting to whiten in streaks, fell forward and to one side, covering an ear and a portion of her thin face. A reviewer at *The New York Times* once wrote on her performance of the *Années de Pèlerinage*, "even Eva Everett's hair performed wonderfully!" This infuriated her. "What insulting nonsense! Hair!"

She stopped playing again, but her head remained tilted. "Now what is it, Amir? I'm sorry but I have so much work to do."

I repeated myself. "This world is a vestibule."

"What of it? Did the Fluchts brainwash you? Maybe you should avoid them." After a pause she added, "If you're going crazy, perhaps you should go live with your father. Punish him. If you can find him."

I had abruptly decided to become a *baal t'shuva*, one who returns to his religious roots. I was repeating something profound I had heard the previous night, something that moved me, suddenly changing my outlook on life. I wanted my mother, in these few words, to feel what I was feeling, a surging desire for a long-sublimated faith. I wanted her to understand what I now understood, that there was something besides this mundane world on which she was so intent.

Finally I said, "And I'll need to reorganize the kitchen. Top to bottom. I can't eat in there anymore."

Actually, my parents were strict vegetarians, so it was practically a moot point. There was never any meat in our house, kosher or otherwise, let alone milk or cheese with which to mix it. I was the one who had always cheated on the outside, sneaking occasional cheeseburgers and frankfurters.

"Do what you want."

I continued to stand there.

"Look," she finally said, "I'm sorry. You *can* do whatever you like. I never said you couldn't. Only don't try to change the way *I* live, okay? That's the only rule."

"Okay."

She raised her right hand, which then came down on a major chord. She repeated this several times, varying the loudness and duration, murmuring and grunting to herself as she did when she was concentrating.

My mother had inadvertently laid the groundwork for my new perspective on life by renting out the cold and airy apartment adjacent to ours, formerly my father's studio, to a young couple. I quickly fell under the spell of these new neighbors, followers, as it turned out, of a famous Hasidic rebbe. They had come to our neighborhood for their rebbe's "Seeds of Torah" movement, through which by good deeds and example the Torah would miraculously germinate in the barren secular soil of the Upper West Side of Manhattan. This sacred mission was considered a full-time job for both husband and wife.

Now, I do not mean by the words "fell under the spell" to imply some witchcraft or deception practiced on their part, as those nonbelievers who always seek to detract from the righteous might prefer, but rather a form of enchantment brought about by the serenity and conviction of their being.

They first appeared to me in the hallway. For a moment I caught myself staring. Paul Flucht was tall, athletic-looking despite his strange dark suit, and, I quickly realized, extremely handsome. His wife, Naomi, slim, barely out of her girlhood, wore elegant suede shoes, dark stockings, and a long dress. Her hair was wrapped in a colorful kerchief that despite its modesty had a flair of fashion and individuality to it. Together they smiled at me and said hello. I nodded shyly and went into my apartment.

One Friday afternoon, a week or so after they moved in, they rang our bell. They stood just outside our doorway. Paul Flucht bowed his head gently. "We would be very honored if you both joined us for dinner tonight."

Naomi Flucht said, "Yes, it would give us great pleasure."

My mother looked at them, smiled broadly, asked them if they had settled in comfortably (she could be very friendly in a stagy manner), and then declined their invitation. "I'm sorry but I have a concert to prepare. Besides, I'm as strict with my vegetarian diet as you people are with yours. I hardly eat anywhere but home. It makes me a bit unsociable, I know." She gave me a strange look. "My son is more flexible."

After they left she said to me, "Careful, everyone is always trying to promote their own gods."

When I went over to the Fluchts' that evening, I stood in wonder in the small foyer of their apartment. The place was dramatically transformed from when my father had used it for his work studio. Heavy velvet drapery hung across the previously unadorned windows, and new plush rugs lay on the wooden floors. There was a soothing warmth in the air and the intoxicating aroma of a nonvegetarian meal. Paul Flucht put his hands on my shoulders and ushered me along. "Welcome, welcome! No need to stand about in the hall, Amir"—he pointed in the direction of the dining area. "Our sages say, 'This world is a vestibule in which we prepare for the glories of Paradise!'"

I was hypnotized by the soft light of the candles set by Naomi Flucht on the far end of a long table covered with white linen. She was smiling and glowed like a candle herself. Their table stood exactly where my father used to work hunched over his composing desk with a glaring lamp and piles of music paper. On one freshly painted wall was a picture of the Fluchts' rebbe with his long beard and mystical eyes. I was transfixed by Paul's harmonious voice when he stood before dinner and sang "Peace to You, Ministering Angels." The sweet melody hovered in the room like a seraph. Paul Flucht seemed the most beautiful person I had ever seen. He took my breath away as his lips formed the unfamiliar words. I knew barely any Hebrew then, as my father never spoke his childhood language. "There is only one language that interests me," my father once told me, "the language of chromatic intervals."

"So, your father is a composer and your mother is a pianist," Paul Flucht mused while we were eating. "A great rebbe once said that music is the purest form of prayer, and prayer is the holy bridge from this world to the next."

His wife smiled and nodded in agreement. She delighted in her husband's words. She went on and explained how everything in the room was imbued with holiness. Even the roast chicken we were eating, she said, "when prepared according to His commandments, is an instrument of serving God, like the sacrifices on the altar of the Temple, may it be restored quickly in our days!" Her husband added, "Even the silverware and china that adorn the table, and the white linen tablecloth, are imbued with holiness in the service and glorification of the Sabbath. The Rebbe always says that everything is transformed to holiness with the joyous intent to serve God. And that is in essence man's duty, to bring about this transformation in our everyday life."

Naomi said, "Oh, I heard a true story that involves music." In the otherworldly light of that evening, Naomi began a complicated tale of a village whose destruction was decreed by God.

How was this decree known?

"In that village there was a great and righteous man, a *tzaddik*, whose soul would ascend every night to heaven during his sleep. One night he overheard God's decree." Naomi folded her delicate hands to her flat chest, lowering her voice. "You know, Amir, the souls of our *tzaddikim* are like those angels in Our Father Yacov's dream. They ascend and descend the ladder that stretches between the earth and heaven. Well anyway, the next morning, after overhearing this terrible news, the *tzaddik* awoke, and of course said the Modeh Ani, 'I am grateful to You, Everlasting King, Who returns each morning my soul in mercy.' The *tzaddik* then prayed fervently day and night, denying himself food and sleep: 'If I have found favor in Your eyes, O Lord, spare our humble village.' But despite his piety and prayers, he was unable to overturn the decree. God simply would not budge."

Naomi cleared her throat, adjusting the kerchief on her head. "Salvation came in a most unexpected way. There happened to be a little boy in the village who was mute. No one paid him any mind, thinking him retarded. He wanted so much to pray to God, but he could not speak. It is a great affliction, you know, not to speak. So what did he do? He whistled a beautiful melody! And when he whistled his heart out, the Gates of Heaven opened and God in His mercy saved the boy's village."

Suddenly I had so many burning questions: "Was the boy praying for his village to be saved? How did he know it was going to be destroyed? Had the *tzaddik* told him about his dream? Were people mean to him? Did they ignore him?"

Naomi took every question seriously. "Oh, no, he wasn't asking for anything. Nobody in town was mean to him. He was simply praying out of love and joy, and that was enough to convince God to abolish His decree. It was a coincidence, really."

Paul revealed another great and illuminating truth: "But then again there is no such thing as a coincidence."

Naomi paused thoughtfully and then smiled at her husband. "So you see, our humblest good deeds can save the world and hasten the coming of the *Moshiach*."

For a moment, catching her smile at her handsome husband, I blushed, for I had the strange and embarrassing thought that I would like to be Naomi.

While we ate dessert, the Fluchts asked what instrument I played.

"I don't play one. I don't have any musical talent," I confessed. "But I'm very good in science. I think it's strange. I know I *look* like my parents, so I guess I'm not adopted. But that's as far as it goes."

"Most people receive a soul from a different root than their parents." Naomi Flucht passed me a second portion of sponge cake. "It's surprising when you think of it, but it's the truth.

And that's probably where our talents really come from. The Rebbe's soul is from the same root as King David's, which of course makes a lot of sense—"

"But where do people's souls come from?" I interrupted with a new river of questions, my heart beating faster and faster. "What is a root? What is the root of my soul? How can you find out?"

This time Naomi laughed. "Oh, Paul knows more about this than I do. He can explain it better."

And then he began to explain, looking inside me with his green eyes. I felt slightly dizzy. I didn't want him to stop looking at me. I tried not to blink too much.

He said, his dark hand absently brushing crumbs on the table, "The repository of souls, the Great Soul from which all souls originate, is likened to the shape of a man, of Adam. When a child is born he is given a soul from one of the myriad parts of Adam. And the part that the soul is taken from, that root, imbues the person with aspects of their personality and talents. I'm not great enough to tell you absolutely for sure where your soul is from, though the Rebbe could. But I would guess that your *neshamah* comes from the eyes of the Great Soul, because you are very perceptive and ask good questions. The eyes are where the prophets and many people of great talent come from." He reached across the table and touched my hand. "Anyway, Amir, I'm sure your soul is special, because I can tell you are a wonderful kid."

I sat astonished. I had goose bumps all over. I had never before given thought to whether I even had a soul, and now the Fluchts had given me a glorious soul on a silver platter. The soul-root of prophets and great talent! The dying flames of the candlesticks flickered, sending up thin and twisting columns of smoke. I suddenly imagined myself ascending like an angel from their table, floating in the heavenly ether, looking out at the most distant stars, and into the most secret of hearts, with the all-seeing eyes of the Great Soul of Man.

One evening, not long after, Gloria asked my mother if she would play my father's Second Piano Concerto with the New York Philharmonic. I feel I should interrupt and digress here to say that my father had always been taken aback, seemingly disappointed by the early and persistent success of his Second Piano Concerto among all the work he produced, as if it were some type of reproach. Nowadays, all these years later, on those rare occasions that I see him, he usually talks about his pieces as if they are his real children and I am some stranger one chats with on an airplane. He has said to me, "Why everyone loves my Second Piano Concerto I'll never know. It is a passionate piece, of course, but not my best. I was too naive when I wrote it. I have since written so many better pieces, my three symphonies for instance, or my violin and flute concertos, pieces whose form make some sense of this world, and these are practically ignored!"

But back on that winter evening, Gloria told my mother that the original pianist engaged to play the Second Piano Concerto would be unable to perform. "I think he has that new disease. He's dreadfully sick." The concert was only a few weeks off.

"I know you may not want to have anything to do with Ivri or his work at this time, Eva. I know you are working on the Strauss and about to start the Poulenc. But I think it would be a good move. You've played this piece before. It's *in* you already."

My mother lowered her voice. "It was *written* for me."

"Yes, I know all that, Eva. But it would be good exposure for you. Mehta is conducting."

My mother looked down at her hands and thought for a moment.

"He's not going to be there, is he?" She paused. "Or she?"

I did not know then what she meant by "she," and did not ask. My mother glanced at me and then at Gloria, who was waiting for her answer.

"No. They're staying in London. I've confirmed that."

"How will I be ready in time?" She squeezed her face between her hands. "I'm going to have to work like a horse!"

In the weeks before the concert I started visiting with the Fluchts more frequently, even on school nights. My mother's practicing of my father's Second Piano Concerto in the evenings was starting to bother me. Neither her playing nor his music had ever disturbed me before. But now the slow first movement seemed to me too whiny, with its meandering repetitions, and the second and third movements cold and angry. And this unexplained anger, as my mother played over and over through the score, seemed to come from both of my parents.

I had never heard my parents really angry until the previous summer, when they had a mysterious argument behind the door of their bedroom. After that it was only a matter of days when my mother made her curt announcement while my father stood back and watched her. He was a head shorter than she was, and though I had, of course, always known and accepted this, I suddenly found this fact disturbing, almost shameful.

"I'm sorry, Amir, but your father and I are not getting along. Your father won't be living with us anymore."

My father said, "I'll speak with you soon and often, son. I'm moving away."

"Where?" I felt all cold inside while I waited for his answer.

"Far away. Europe." He was looking at my mother, not at me.

I walked out of the room. I never asked any other questions, and my mother did not bring up the subject again. The next day my father was gone. I did not see him or even speak to him for several years.

Sometimes I wonder why I did not ask any more questions at that crucial moment, if only out of my strong sense of curiosity. But I remember a stubborn, mechanical voice in my head that repeated, "Do not ask. Do not care. Do not ask. Do not care."

Perhaps, I tell myself now, I did not want to know anything. It was too painful. I loved my father. How could he leave me? But I convinced myself that I did not care and I did not ask.

And so it was a long time before I fully understood how my father had fallen in love with a young composer, an Englishwoman, a former student of his, and had moved to London to be near her.

During those intense weeks while my mother was relearning my father's Second Piano Concerto, I learned many things from the Fluchts. I studied the letters of the *aleph-bais*, from which God had created the world out of nothingness. I heard how the child Abraham had destroyed all the statues in his father Terach's idol shop. When his father angrily asked what happened, Abraham calmly said, "You believe they are living gods, don't you? Well, these living gods fought and destroyed one another." And I acquired a rudimentary knowledge of the Sabbath laws. I stopped going to movies or watching television on that lofty day. I waited until Sunday to do my written homework. But even as I sat and learned and drank in the serene atmosphere of their apartment and words, I could faintly hear my mother's practicing coming from next door.

"It's starting to drive me crazy, listening to all that," I told the Fluchts one evening.

"You sound upset, Amir," Naomi said gently. "You should never be upset with your mother for working so hard. The Torah commands us to honor our parents. And besides, it's always so beautiful to hear someone playing the piano."

"Yes," her husband added. "Remember, we once talked about music being close to prayer."

Naomi started to retell the story of the whistling boy but Paul raised his eyebrows. She stopped and rolled her eyes. "Oh, I've told that one already, haven't I? Did I tell you how the Rebbe once stopped in the street to learn a hymn of God's praise from the sparrows?"

Increasingly the Fluchts had other people over, too. Their Seeds of Torah mission was starting to have some minor success. I would try to hide my disappointment if someone was already there when I came over. A heavy college student named Cassandra, the daughter of a reform rabbi, started coming by frequently. Most of her conversations centered on her inability to believe in God.

"I don't find believing in God useful to me," she would say addressing Naomi, or, "Why does He need to have *me* believe in *Him*? What's *His* problem?"

Naomi Flucht said, "That's not why we believe, Cassandra. We don't do it for Him or to benefit ourselves, though it's good for us, of course. God doesn't need us to believe in Him. That's not the point."

"What is?" She would become all red in the face.

"To serve and love God. To be closer to Him and help perfect our world. That's all."

"Well, that's a tall order! It still doesn't make sense to me. I just can't help *not* believing in Him."

Paul Flucht, intervening, spoke patiently, sweetly, while Cassandra fidgeted with her napkin: "Sometimes we do believe but just cannot admit it to ourselves. Otherwise why are you so concerned with the whole question?" He laughed gently. "'Methinks she doth protest too much.'"

Cassandra nodded. She stared at Paul, her eyes glazing over. "Well, maybe . . ."

Later, after Cassandra left, the Fluchts took me into their confidence. Naomi said, "I think Cassandra is beginning to understand, Paul. Deep down she has a pure and wonderful *neshamah.*"

Paul said, "I think so, too. What do you think, Amir? You're the perceptive one."

A few days before the performance of my father's Second Piano Concerto my mother took me aside. I had just come home from school. We had barely spoken a word during the last weeks.

"Amir, why don't you invite the Fluchts to come to the concert? I have plenty of comps."

"They won't be able to come. It's a Friday night."

My mother rolled her eyes. "Oh, I forgot. The Holy Sabbath. I guess your new friends think coming to my concert is a sin. Well, are you coming?"

Her question upset me greatly. Until that moment it had never occurred to me not to go. I always went to my mother's concerts when they were in town. I may have given the impression that my mother was never attentive or enthusiastic about me. But this was not the case when she just finished a performance. She was happiest after playing a concert and always engulfed me in her joy and love in a way she was never capable of at home.

"Do you all know my wonderful Amir?" she would say, standing tall and elegant in the green room as her line of admirers approached, or if someone congratulated her on a wonderful performance, she might say, "Amir here is my greatest success. Look how he's growing!"

"Well," she repeated, "are you coming?"

I surprised myself with my answer, by its firmness and finality.

"No. I won't be able to go either."

My mother's face paled. She trembled almost imperceptibly. But then she said flatly, faintly, as she turned to leave the room, "You can do whatever you want, Amir."

I was surprised at the Fluchts' agitation, and what seemed truly like sorrow, when I told them what had happened.

"But you must go, Amir. She'll be so disappointed," Naomi said. She was close to tears.

Paul spoke nervously, he nibbled his thumbnail. He no longer seemed beautiful to me. "Remember, 'Honor your mother and father.' You could walk to the concert hall, Amir. It's not that far. You don't have to ride. Your mother could leave you a ticket there, I'm sure, so you won't have to carry money."

"Will you come with me?"

"No, we couldn't, really. . . . It's different with us . . ." they said in unison.

"Well, then I shouldn't be going either." I was filling up with an uncontrollable stubbornness, but I couldn't help it.

"You're trying to change too quickly," Paul said. "You have a whole life of serving God ahead of you. Remember, Amir, we still live in this world, and with our loved ones, too."

I said I had to leave to do my homework.

That night I dreamed Paul Flucht was floating before me. I saw his face and then his athletic arms and legs swaying in the weightlessness and I understood that he was the Great Soul and my soul rose out of the naked parts of his soul, but I could not tell from which. My soul tried to float toward his soul, but could not. I had other dreams, too, that night, rich and mystical dreams that seemed to last for eons, but I could not remember them.

When I awoke I was full of a great and painful longing. And it occurred to me, in the midst of this yearning that I did not understand, and feared might never leave me, that I would, and somehow must, cling to my stubbornness. I was angry, too, at my mother, though I knew she had done nothing wrong. What could she do to help me? Still I could not help myself. And when I came home that Friday afternoon from school, and the evening of the concert arrived, I did not change my mind.

I did not go to my mother's concert and I never went back to the Fluchts'.

While my mother was out playing my father's Second Piano Concerto, I went early to my room so I could pretend I was asleep when she came back. When she finally came home, somewhat earlier than I had expected, I heard a knock on my door and was surprised when I heard Gloria's voice call my name. She came into my room, closed the door, and sat on the edge of my bed in the dark. She lit a cigarette. "Do you mind, Amir?"

"No."

"Well, this is the story."

She told me how my father had lied to her and had flown in from England to hear his Second Piano Concerto. "What a desperate ego!" She told me how he even went up on stage to take a bow and how my mother, from the shock of seeing him, trembled slightly but fought successfully to maintain her composure before the audience. "I could tell right away how upset she was, but of course I know her like I know myself. I don't think anyone else could tell. But I had to take her straight home. She didn't even go to the green room. And she had just given the most stunning performance I can remember!"

Gloria began weeping. "I feel so awful, Amir. I was the one who assured her that your father would not be there. I'm sorry to tell you these things. You're still a kid. But it has all devastated your mother. She has put up such a good show for so long. But your mother did love Ivri despite his failings. One doesn't get over such things so easily. Love is not something we can control. I'm sure you know that. Why don't you just come out and see her. It will be good for her. You don't have to say anything. Really. Just go to her."

And so I went out to the living room. My mother was sitting very still on the sofa. Her eyes were red and her dark hair with its growing white streaks hung limp around the sides of her face. She nodded at me but we did not speak. I sat beside her. I took her hand in mine and held it for what seemed the longest time.

It occurred to me then, as I sat there with my mother's hand in my own, that in the next days I might hear from my father, that he would try to contact me somehow, but he never did.

In a few days my mother seemed herself. She was rehearsing her Strauss again and began working on Poulenc's Piano Concerto in C-sharp Minor, which she had never played before and was engaged to perform the following season.

I did not ask any questions when she told me in a matter-of-fact tone that the Fluchts would be leaving the rented apartment at the end of the month. In those final days I continued to avoid the Fluchts, but before they moved for good I chanced upon them one last time in the hallway. They stopped and said shyly, "Hello, Amir. How are you?" They seemed very sad, as if they had wanted so much to talk to me, but I found I could not bear to even glance at them. I was polite, though, and answered, my eyes lowered to the floor. "Hello, I'm fine. Thank you."

And in those fleeting moments, my eyes cast down at the patterned tiles below me, I felt the faint knowledge of prophecy. I knew I would always look back to that vanishing time, to the shining faith of the Fluchts, and to my mother's uncontrollable love, which was the source of her musical life.

THE DIALOGUES
OF TIME AND ENTROPY

❧   ❧   ❧

"Who are you? Who are you?" Christine's eyes oscillated sideways. She was sixteen, blond, and very thin. Supported by her parents, she walked unsteadily across our reception area into the examining room. She sent out her hand as if to touch me, but her arm flapped about like a wing. "Who are you? Oh, yes, I think I know. . . . Oh, yes, I know. Stop flying, I can hardly see you!"

"Are we all flying, Christine?" I asked as her parents helped her into a chair.

"No, only you, silly! I'm down here." For a moment she seemed perplexed. "I don't know. Everyone is moving so fast. We must all be flying. What?" She turned and tried to focus on her mother, then again on me. "Who are you?"

187

Her mother started crying. "Tell us the truth, doctor. Where did this sickness come from? Two weeks ago she was completely normal. An honor student. She went to the prom!"

"We really don't know," I answered. "We think it's an infectious agent, perhaps a new virus, perhaps—"

I accidentally dropped my pen. Christine jumped out of her seat and screamed. "Oh, my God, a bomb!" She then fell back exhausted into the chair, closing her eyes. Her violent reaction to my pen hitting the floor occurred despite other, louder noises that she didn't seem to notice: doors closing in the hall, traffic outside rumbling past the institute.

"We hope we will have an experimental treatment soon, in the next few months," I continued, trying to sound hopeful. I had just laboriously synthesized the first aliquots of reverse polymerase, a theoretical antidote but a still-untested treatment.

"She needs help now, not in a few months! You know that!" her father shouted.

Dr. Schpizhof, head of the Neurological Institute, with whom I worked, finally spoke, raising his hand. "Sir, of course we know that. Please be calm."

The father softened his voice and pleaded. "Please help her. Please."

While they spoke, Christine opened her eyes and looked at me, her blue eyes oscillating up and down. "Who are you? Oh, yes, I know. Come down here! You'll go through the ceiling!"

Dr. Schpizhof took me outside the examining room. "It's time, Paul. It's time. We cannot watch this poor girl deteriorate. It's still early and we must try our best. A more-than-willing patient and family! We must go ahead now. We must! We must!"

Schpizhof had been the first to recognize the twenty-eight-case cluster of a terrifying new dementia that appeared three summers before throughout Ontario. All of the patients either died or rapidly progressed to a vegetative state. At first he called the new syndrome "the unzipping disease" because under the electron microscope the neuronal junctions in parts of the brain looked frayed and separated—unzipped. In the span of one year Schpizhof had performed the incredible feat of isolating a certain protein polymerase found in damaged areas of victims' brains. But he could not determine—nor had anyone yet—the actual causative agent or mode of transmission.

"Paul, we have no other choice. You know what will happen if we do nothing. Remember, a new disease is an unparalleled opportunity for knowledge. We have no other leads," Schpizhof said.

I hesitated. A new disease, like a newly discovered animal species or a newly discovered subatomic particle, is also an opportunity for the reevaluation of unquestioned beliefs and for confusion. The reverse polymerase I had designed worked perfectly in the computer model, locking its own three-dimensional structure with that of the polymerase, presumably neutralizing it. But we did not even know whether the polymerase was indeed the offending agent or simply a by-product. And there was still no experimental animal model. Computers, after all, could never fully duplicate the great molecular sea of the brain.

Schpizhof grabbed my arm. "Paul, please listen to me. I have already obtained Compassionate Release for her from the government. The father is a minister of Parliament. Didn't you know? Even so, it wasn't easy. I went to great trouble. All taken care of. There is no other choice but to go ahead. We have to do something, don't you agree? She is a human being, a person. You must not forget that."

And later he solemnly told the parents in the examining room, "You will have to sign this. Read it carefully. It is an experimental protocol. We are very fortunate to have received approval. Remember, there are no guarantees. We will admit her to University Hospital tonight."

Christine's parents bowed their heads silently.

Once, before she left, when my wife and I were quarreling over our daughter Nona, my wife said calmly, "I know now where the seed comes from. From you. You fall in love with inanimate phrases, ideas, disembodied molecules, but you are indifferent— or I should say more accurately, do not relate—to people, to living things, to our own daughter. That is the root of her isolation." But in defense against this harsh evaluation, I explained that I was indeed capable of love: "Did I not fall in love with you?"

"Perhaps, perhaps only with my ideas, my head, my little book," she said.

I tried to explain myself. That I was incapable of false hope, which is often confused with love or faith. "After all," I argued, "with a book one does not expect to be loved back, though with living things one hopes for a response."

"But I've always loved you."

"I know that. I meant Nona."

"How are we different? I am her mother. If I love you, she loves you. So, *a fortiori,* you must not love me."

Ahuva was brilliant, but she made no sense to me.

It is true, in a limited sense, that I may have fallen in love with my wife, long before we met, by proxy, through the exhilarating personification of Time, whom Ahuva had introduced in the guise of a beautiful, sensuous countess moving through her garden, "a fragrant paradise of great symmetry," with her suitor, the handsome, heartsick Entropy. When Entropy arrives, he shyly hands Time a rose, "a pale and romantic damask," and begins the haunting stream of exchanges that frame the brilliant essays of Ahuva's book.

I had first read *The Dialogues of Time and Entropy* when I was in medical school. It was something of a phenomenon, a slim fairy tale of a book by a distinguished young physicist studying in Paris. Penrose called it "a delightful parable in the tradition of Fontenelle, a magic window whose poetic clarity reveals, for the lay and professional alike, the quantum underpinnings of our universe."

But the accolades were not what drew me to the book at first—rather, that the author's last name was the familiar and revered Adayim.

In my teens, as a yeshiva student, I had read the erudite *History of the Spheres* and *God in the Shards of Time,* by Enoch Adayim, the great scholar of mystical texts. I was drawn to the hidden latticework of a holy, magisterial universe that supported our flimsy, ephemeral world, making it more solid, making it purposeful, unique. The ancient weave of dream and myth gave me solace.

So years later, when I was in medical school and saw Ahuva's book reviewed in *The Globe and Mail,* I thought, "She is Adayim's daughter. I must read this."

> *Time and Entropy sat in the garden awaiting the sunset. Entropy, jittery and given to melancholy, saw the liquid, ruby sphere of light reflected in his beloved's blue eyes. He lit a cigarette and sighed.*
>
> *"You are so quiet. Please, talk to me," Entropy implored Time. "I cherish every word."*
>
> *"But don't you find"—she smiled, holding up the fragrant rose he had given her—"that words are useless for conveying one's deepest thoughts?"*

I cannot remember who—it seems now the Finger of God itself—pointed out Ahuva's small figure in the university's synagogue. "Do you know who that is?" I recall not spoken words but writing on the chapel walls in letters of light.

Ahuva had arrived at the university after I had already received my medical degree and doctorate in neurochemistry. I had done some very promising work on protein folding and the three-dimensional structure of neurotransmitters. I was given my own lab. Ahuva was invited from Paris to chair the division of theoretical physics, presumably on the strength of her work on space-time singularities, though no doubt the commercial success and popular fame of *The Dialogues* made her irresistible to the search committee.

I was thirty. Ahuva, standing in the half-light of the chapel, looked like a skinny high school student, not a rising pillar of the scientific world, a woman of forty. She was green-eyed, her thick dark hair in a long ponytail. As I watched her gently swaying in prayer, all common hesitations, all doubts about myself receded beneath the romantic pull of Time and the erotic tide of Entropy.

I nervously introduced myself after services, never having done such a thing before. Until then I had managed to go through university keeping to myself, as if the only things in the world were my protein structures, my computer simulators. I had kept away from people and decided upon a research career rather than a clinical career. In the years since my father had died—even before, in the silent years of a motherless childhood—I had become used to my small sphere of loneliness, accustomed to its hard, invisible shell.

After I introduced myself, I was quickly at ease. Ahuva was chatty, familiar. Her words filled the empty sphere around me.

"Well, if you read my little book," she said smiling, glancing back as we left the synagogue, "you could guess I have never been able to grasp reality, let alone religion. Why, I do not see why we cannot walk through walls! But I still believe in prayer, even if I really don't understand the 'to whom,' and miracles, even if I don't understand how, and other dimensions of existence, even if I don't know where. I guess it's my upbringing. You know, when my father died he said, 'Ahuvale, stay with me so I don't fall down there.' Crazy as it sounds, I looked under his deathbed as if it might be straddling his grave. But please, forgive me, I'm babbling"—she touched my arm—"please, tell me who you are again."

Entropy stood in the rose bower at twilight, a puzzled look on his face.

"What is it, my dear?" Time asked.

"Here," Entropy said, gently caressing her arm, "you are olive-skinned and brunette, yet I recall a fairer skin, earlier, in the orchard, and blond hair in the afternoon light."

"Oh, but it all depends upon your point of view. I'm different in different places. No doubt you will find me blond again when we walk about."

"It saddens me that I never met your father," I told Ahuva after we first made love. Sibelius's Violin Concerto was playing on her phonograph. My heart was still rapidly beating. My unexpected feeling of loss surprised me. I knew it wasn't just the music. I told Ahuva how I had read her father's books more than fifteen years earlier when I was a yeshiva student. I felt as if I were holding something back by not telling her about my own sensation, never far away, of being enclosed and set apart from the natural world.

"He would have liked you, I'm sure." Ahuva smiled. "I do. Father loved brilliance, whatever field it was in. And your work is amazing—I've always believed, and I've mentioned this in an essay, that the configurations of organic molecules and the pulsing structures of galaxies all imply a universe of broken symmetries, the self-similar organizing principles of a universe on the way to equilibrium. Anyway, pure symmetry is a sterile type of beauty, don't you think?" She divided her face with her finger and smiled. "Look, I'm asymmetric!"

I laughed. Her fine nose and her smile were very slightly crooked. I suppose most people would have found her plain.

Still, lying there beside me, she was beautiful, comfortable, familiar. I gently moved her finger away from her face and clasped it in my hand.

"I still remember your father's words, how the mystics imposed a 'template for the illusion of the world.'"

"'For the *frail substance* of the world,'" Ahuva corrected me with a smile. "I don't think he thought the world was an illusion. Perhaps our image of it is, how we see it. But not the world itself."

"What made you write the *Dialogues?*"

"The idea came to me in a dream. Do you ever get ideas from dreams?" She caressed my shoulder. "Now I always keep a notebook handy near my bed. One night I dreamed I was arguing some point, I can't remember what, and I became intimidated by some presence. It was Time. She was a person! She was so beautiful, so lovely and articulate." Ahuva smiled to herself. "My father, not long before he became ill, read the manuscript and urged me to publish it. I never expected it would be so popular."

"Well, it's more than popular, it's brilliant, like you. Just think if we have children—they'll be so smart."

"Children?" She sounded surprised. She looked in my eyes to see if I meant it. I remember her green eyes just then as if I had never seen anyone's eyes before. I had never thought about eyes before. "Yes, children," I said, though I may have sounded frightened. What if she refused me? She turned her head and held me tight, I could feel the fine bones beneath her skin. "Oh, wonderful," she said, and her own rapid heartbeat fluttered against my chest.

The original cluster of polymerase dementia cases flared the summer Nona was born. Fall, winter, and spring followed with no new cases. It was during this period that Schpizhof isolated the polymerase. When summer came around again, everyone feared a new outbreak. Many people left the city and even the province. From time to time that summer, unfounded rumors spread of new cases.

Schpizhof came unannounced to my laboratory. "I'm very impressed with your computer-generated studies of neuro-chemical structure. Extraordinary!"

Schpizhof had a plan. He did not know if the polymerase he found in the brain was a distracting artifact, a by-product of the dementing agent, or a mediating link in the damaging process. He wanted to determine the three-dimensional structure of the polymerase and design a blocking agent. The polymerase was all he had to go on. If a blocking agent could be designed, we might determine the role of the polymerase and perhaps have a treatment.

"Remember, a new disease is an unparalleled opportunity for knowledge!" Schpizhof's voice lowered. "Perhaps this cluster was all a fluke, but maybe the disease will return, unexpectedly, in its own time cycle, and worse, more widespread than before. Paul, I'm counting on you to help me."

Let me explain here that biological molecules—amino acids, sugars, whatever—when strung together, come alive through their structure. They stand up and reach out with their chemical limbs. And in the computer, one can calculate or at least approximate the way biomolecules will bend in a cytoplasmic lake, the way they will grab hold of one another or be received. After two years of collaboration and work, only three years after the original case cluster, we were ready to publish our findings, a computer-designed complex protein strand synthesized in our laboratory, a *reverse* polymerase, I called it, and a possible antidote for the polymerase dementia.

They came to a garden terrace where stood a grand piano. Rows of orange daylilies grew on every side, their blooms open in the night.

"They are enchanted by the full moon," Time told Entropy, "and believe she is their sun."

Time sat down and played a fantasy piece by Schumann. Entropy closed his eyes, his heart filling with a sweet and intense nostalgia. He prayed the music would never stop. But it quickly ended, and Entropy opened his eyes. Time rose, her gown rustling. She bowed gently, in the glorious cone of a moonbeam.

Entropy was about to ask for an encore, but the great instrument was now nowhere to be seen. "But the piano . . . the music?" His voiced quavered. Bewildered, he stretched out his arm tentatively, uncertain now even of Time.

"Oh, forgive me." Time placed her hand firmly in his. "I have always endeavored to eschew illusion, but have not yet succeeded."

When Nona was born, Ahuva and I could not believe our good fortune. She was beautiful. Exquisite. She slept quietly through the night, fed regularly and conveniently. I was, for all of Ahuva's later pronouncements, happy to be a father, overjoyed.

Ahuva's involvement with the baby was intense. She had taken to placing a bow in the few soft blond curls atop the baby's head, which made Nona look like a cartoon baby but was really an attempt to copy a look Ahuva had in the sole remaining baby picture of herself. There, with a similar bow in her hair, she lay on a table, smiling, holding her little feet. "Doesn't she look like I did?" she said, handing me the picture. I think it is honest to say we were both happy in our new parenthood, even with all the frightening changes taking place in the natural world.

Ahuva's routine was little affected by the baby's arrival. After all, her work and research were theoretical. She was paid to think, and this she could do anywhere. She would sit near a window in the living room, nursing Nona and looking all the way out to the ends of the universe and time. But after several months it slowly became apparent that everything was not right with our baby. Nona did not smile as other babies did. She could see, we knew, and would follow bright objects, a red rattle or the colorful mobile of tropical birds above her crib. But she did not see us. She never looked in our direction. We were invisible. One day I found Ahuva holding her and crying. "She doesn't know me, and nothing we know can help her!" For a while we took her from specialist to specialist. At first they said, "You must give her time, it is too early to say what all this means," and later, as Nona's dissociation became more apparent, they said, "You must not expect much. Perhaps, with intensive work . . . perhaps . . ." When Nona was eighteen months old she would sit on the floor, for hours sometimes, just holding a chair leg or clutching a piece of string. "She needs more attention," Ahuva would say, "to help her break through. Maybe she will respond one day and I won't be there."

Ahuva thought Nona might respond to music; there were many famous, well-documented cases of autistic children who could play instruments. Ahuva bought a piano and took up playing again. None of this, however, seemed to work or to capture Nona's attention. Ahuva would play and Nona would sit motionless on the floor or in her little chair, the only object for which she seemed to have an attachment.

At first, Ahuva still went to the university on occasion to give her lectures or attend an academic meeting. But by the time Nona was two, Ahuva would not leave the house at all. She sat around watching Nona. She stopped her research. She lost all interest. She played the piano infrequently, listlessly. I was angry with her for allowing herself an intellectual decline. I thought she should see someone, but she refused. When I came home from the lab I now found her reading books like *Your Heart, Your Mind* or *Your Guide to Interpreting the Stars.*

"I know what you're thinking," she said to me once when I caught her reading *The Astral Influence.*

"Oh, really? What?"

"You know what," she said, smiling sadly. "I can tell from your aura."

By this time, my work on the reverse polymerase was in high gear. I had mapped out the amino acid sequence and, more crucially, its cross-linkage and three-dimensional structure. These were the first steps in designing a blocking agent. My days stretched into the evenings, sometimes even into the early hours of the morning. Often when I came home I found Ahuva watching the cable news in our bedroom while Nona sat in a corner staring at the wall.

It was on CNN that we first saw a short feature on the settlement of Tuval. Prefabricated homes were parading by on flatbed trucks, then being lifted and lowered by cranes onto a high plateau. On one side of the plateau were towering wind turbines, tall, whirring prophets surveying the wilderness from white concrete pedestals. Later, after Ahuva left, these images would come to me in dreams. Sometimes I, too, was standing among the turbines, surveying the wilderness or pulling the great flatbed trucks with my own sunburned hands.

"Ahuva," I interrupted, "I think I'm almost—"

"Wait, shhh." Ahuva waved at me.

A reporter was talking: "The settlers come from all walks of life, doctors, lawyers, farmers, from all parties and ideologies, but they have in common their own unique rapport with the world. They believe in miracles."

"The kabbalists knew," Ahuva said, turning her green eyes to me, "that we are all interchangeable with energy."

"Ahuva, this is all going too far. I think you're having a nervous breakdown." I walked backward and stood outside the bedroom door.

Ahuva turned off the television with the remote control. She came over to the doorway, smiled, and kissed me for the first time in many months. "No, Paul. Actually, I'm not having any such thing. Not anymore." And she led me back into the bedroom.

A few evenings later I called Ahuva from my lab to tell her that I would be working late. That was the day I made a major breakthrough in designing the reverse polymerase. "Now I'm really on to something, Ahuva. I just can't stop. And Schpizhof will be amazed."

"That's nice." She sounded distracted.

When I came home at sunrise, Ahuva was in her nightgown, getting breakfast for Nona in the kitchen. Nona always awoke at dawn.

"You know, Paul, there are some places, times, dimensions, 'singularities'"—Ahuva was pouring a bowl of cereal for Nona—"that are outside the usual physical laws of nature. This is not religious pseudoscience. Haven't you read my monograph *Space-Time Irregularities*? Anyway, you know I grew up and lived in Jerusalem until I left for France!" Her voice still carried the faintest of childhood accents. "We could even see the territories from my father's study. 'Someday, someday,' my father would say looking out, 'we may live there too.'"

"Has your brain been sucked into a black hole?"

"Look, Paul, we could all go together. I'm sure you could do your work there. I know the chairman of the National Foundation. He was a great admirer of my—"

We were interrupted by Nona, who threw her bowl off the breakfast table and shrieked as if she had been stabbed. It was an unnerving sound from such a small child. Ahuva had mistakenly given Nona Special K instead of Frosted Flakes.

"You know you're not supposed to change the slightest

component of her routine, her food, even her *spoon.* And now you want to move with her thousands of miles away?"

"She'll adjust. She'll get better. She's not a robot."

"How can you tell?"

"You're the only robot around here." Ahuva marched zombie-like across the kitchen, arms outstretched in front of her. "I am robot scientist. Bleep. Bleep. Work. Work. Ignore family." She went over to Nona, who was now whimpering.

"Don't depend on miracles," I said.

"Why not? I believe in them," Ahuva insisted. "And I've finally made up my mind. I'm leaving Canada with Nona."

"Look, I've got to lie down. I've been up all night. I haven't given up *my* work, yet."

"I'm not giving up either, Paul." She stood there, her slender arms crossed. "Really, I hope you understand."

The following week they were gone. I never thought she'd actually leave. Then I thought she'd be back in no time.

I was mistaken.

Now, after a year of living in the settlement, by virtue of her prominence both as a physicist and as the daughter of Enoch Adayim, she had become an ideologue, a sort of ambassador-at-large. She wrote papers, quasi-scientific and otherwise. She gave interviews. She had even led demonstrations in front of Parliament.

Christine's response was amazing. Through a spinal puncture, Dr. Schpizhof instilled the small amount of the reverse polymerase I had synthesized. "May I do the honors, Paul?" he said, drawing up the solution into a syringe. He was very gentle. First he gave Christine a mild sedative. One had to be careful, because some classes of sedatives and tranquilizers agitated patients with polymerase dementia. "A little mosquito bite," he said, and the spinal needle was in place.

Dr. Schpizhof hired a cameraman to videotape Christine's progress twenty-four hours a day. "The three rules of great science"—he laughed—"are document, document, document." In a few days, Christine began walking steadily, without assistance, around her hospital room. Her ocular oscillations ceased.

"Are you flying now?" Schpizhof asked her in front of the video camera. He raised his gray eyebrows and affected a slightly British accent.

"No. Are you?" She was annoyed by the question.

"How do you feel?" Dr. Schpizhof asked as she walked toward the lens.

"I feel like I've been away for a long time. I feel like everything has finally slowed down to normal."

"Well, now you're back."

"Yes, back."

The following day Christine continued to improve. All her movements were smoother, more coordinated. She would smile shyly. "Just like her old self," her mother said.

Schpizhof would not yet allow the news media to interview Christine, but he did release the videotapes of the promising initial phase of her recovery. These scenes were broadcast on CNN along with the video of Christine before her treatment, her limbs flapping, screaming, "Who are you? Come down!" On the seventh day of her recovery Schpizhof allowed her to talk with the growing crowd of reporters waiting at the Neu-rological Institute. He allowed them five minutes with her in the solarium. "How do you feel?" they asked. Christine smiled very shyly. "Oh, much better, thank you. The doctors say I'm much better, too, but I'm still a little tired." She slowly brushed a lock of blond hair from her face.

After the reporters left, Dr. Schpizhof could not contain himself. He slapped me on the back. "The Nobel Prize for sure, my boy!" I was feeling happy, too. Though I'd worked so hard on it, I had never believed the treatment would work so well or so fast. I thought I should call Ahuva at the settlement to tell her, but I decided not to. Instead Ahuva called me.

"Congratulations! I saw your great success on television. I'm really proud of you. Maybe now you'll have time to leave your work and visit us."

"We'll see. I don't think I should leave just now. This is only the beginning. You know, Ahuva, I don't understand why you want me or need me. Really I don't. It doesn't make sense."

"First of all I love you."

"Well, I mean if you really want to see me, why don't *you* come back? Miracles can happen here, too."

"Not the kind Nona needs."

The following morning, reporters were waiting outside my house. "Doctor, can you tell us how you are feeling today about the miraculous cure you and Dr. Schpizhof have produced?"

"But I don't believe in miracles," I said. "I believe in sci-ence." Which I suppose was a dull thing to say.

⚜

There is something people have asked me, a question I have indeed asked myself. How did I get into this field of complex folding molecules, three-dimensional chemical savants that tell neurons when to grow or die, to stretch and branch this way or that, to signal and transmit, to join together in galactic numbers, to think or love or express their will? I cannot do any better than to say that I have stumbled each step of the way.

Ahuva would insist that in me, though not in her own parallel scientific and theoretical pursuits, these rarefied and esoteric plottings, these obsessions with such microscopic things, were an attempt to escape from facing real life. "My work," she would say, "draws me outward beyond myself into space and time, while you, Paul, look closer and closer inward. On a molecular level." A trait, she believed, I transmitted to Nona, a thousand-fold, through the relentless and unfortunate double helices of my chromosomes. It did not matter to Ahuva that autism was never proven to be a genetic disease. "Please understand," Ahuva would say, "I'm not really blaming you. You are as much a victim as she."

Time suggested a game. "Cover your eyes, then count until you're ready."

She hurried into the privet maze that spread out over the southern lawn of her château. Once hidden deep inside, she stood very still as if this might make her invisible.

Entropy, slightly out of breath, was soon behind her. "I've found you. What will my reward be?" His voice was plaintive.

Time, faintly blushing, fleetingly revealed that soft and marvelous infinity enclosed within her summer gown.

Entropy grew with desire and, clumsily, tried to draw her into his arms.

Time, laughing, held him back. "We have the whole evening before us!" And she disappeared again into the maze.

Why didn't I just follow Ahuva and move to the settlement, bide my time with her until she realized her folly?

I could not.

I had become deeply convinced of an emanating history that touched upon my own life. I was given the opportunity to do something with all my training that might be dramatic, perhaps immortal. I had long been coming to the conclusion, though until now I did not expect anything more, that I could not bear simply to produce yet another intellectual drop—a molecule analyzed, a star discovered, a gene identified—to be added and dispersed in the vast ocean of scientific knowledge. I knew there was some reason for the small lonely sphere that had held me apart, for its hard invisible shell, some secret preparation within. And the time, it seemed, for me to think clearly, to work objectively, to achieve something worthy, had come.

On the tenth day following her treatment, we were walking Christine and her parents to the solarium. Suddenly she began screaming, "Oh, my head! My head!" Her eyes rolled up. She collapsed on the floor, her body shaking, her head and limbs banging against the linoleum. She lost bowel control. There was an awful stench.

I vomited.

"For God's sake!" Schpizhof screamed at me. He turned

to the cameraman, who was focusing on the crumpled body. "Turn that damn thing off and help us carry her!"

A magnetic resonance scan showed small hemorrhages scattered throughout the temporal lobes of the brain. She went into a coma.

Christine was placed on a respirator. I knew it might be only days or perhaps a few weeks before she died. Another protein, resembling my reverse polymerase, flashed in my head, a rare and poorly understood protein from an Amazonian eel that I had read about once in graduate school. A powerful anticoagulant. In that instant, I saw that other protein spin around and then superimpose itself on my reverse polymerase, identical except for one chemical arm. I shuddered at their similarity and thought, Perhaps that is why Christine bled into her brain. I knew she was doomed even if we had not treated her, but I could not stop thinking that I had killed her.

I felt the eyes of the whole, heavy, spaceborne world upon me.

"Well, it's true. Miracles *are* happening every day," Ahuva insisted. Lately, in the middle of the night, she was haranguing me from halfway across the globe, at dawn in her world. She had become almost desperate since my troubles began. "It's true. Come see for yourself. And now the government is . . . Hello? What? . . ."

I yawned loudly—the last two weeks I'd been needing ten milligrams of Valium to help me sleep—and her voice flickered off, then on again. I knew this had something to do with sound switches, the traffic bouncing off satellites, and the vast distance between us.

"Paul, are you there? Talk . . ."

"Right now, Ahuva, I could use some miracles myself. And some sleep."

"Well, come then. Miracles are *contagious*. They *snowball*. And really you should see Nona. I know I've taken her far away, but she *is* your daughter. ("I'm sorry," she had said the day she left, smoothing her dark hair with her hand. "But I cannot sit around with my daughter—" "Our daughter," I corrected her. "You're right, I'm glad you finally said that. I cannot sit around with *our* daughter, a hopeless captive of your fatalistic view of the universe.")

"Paul, something is about to happen to Nona. A light is about to go on. And this is the place for it to happen. This is why I came here. I know we've been through this over and over. But now with this terrible new government initiative . . . Anyway, a daughter should know her father. . . ."

"She's autistic. She wouldn't know if I were there or not."

"How can you say that? How do you know what's going on in her mind?"

We were repeating old arguments.

"Ahuva, why did you move thousands of miles away?"

"You have your visions and I have mine."

"Why don't you come back, work on something useful, your scientific theories, for example, instead of lost causes."

"Define 'useful.' It all depends on your point of view. The symmetry of time and the universe? Aperiodic quasi crystals? The latticework of chaos? Blah, blah, blah? It all drives me crazy. I'm sick of it. What I am doing is scientific and *useful*, though the parameters may be hidden in a quantum fog."

"Don't depend on miracles."

"I'm not *depending*. I'm just stating facts."

Indeed there were recent reports of miracles, or phenomena, depending on your point of view, in the settlement Ahuva left me to join: sightings of thought-to-be-extinct biblical birds, peculiar trends in the weather, and recently an explosive vegetal fertility.

Suddenly Ahuva's voice on the phone was insistent. I was starting to drift off to sleep. I had lost her train of thought. "Paul, are you there? I am not claiming to be a prophetess. The government is just trying to make me out to be crazy. The self-organization within chaos and islands of symmetrical time are not prophecies!"

"Ahuva, I've lost you completely. I can't concentrate. I have other things on my mind. I have to get some sleep."

"Oh, how is your antipolymerase treatment working? How is your patient? Really, how is the girl?"

"Worse every day. I'd rather not talk about it. Waiting for the inevitable is torture. I suppose I deserve . . ."

"Torture? . . . Well, now you know how I feel with this crazy new government initiative. I'm racking my brains about it. And everything is happening so quickly. Everything is in a spin. It's crazy! It's making me dizzy!"

"It's not the same," I said. "You're playing a very dangerous . . ."

"Me dangerous? Look, Paul, let's not have this conversation right now. Maybe when you're rested."

"I don't see how that . . ."

But Ahuva had already hung up, leaving my sentence to disintegrate somewhere in space.

After that I could not sleep well, even with the Valium. I dreamed again of my reverse polymerase. My terrible catastrophe. My unremitting nightmare. That infinitesimal protein, a sequence of eight amino acids that I had designed in the laboratory, came hurtling out of empty space, a chain of bloody cannonballs, accompanied by a loud piercing sound, part train whistle, part Nona's murder-victim shriek. I fled across the sky in terror.

Waking up, soaked with sweat, I thought of Ahuva's "strange singularity," as she might call it: her upbringing by a great scholar of mysticism ("What else could I have become but a physicist or a kabbalist!"), her magnificent brain, the searing self-isolation of our daughter Nona, and the unpredictable locale of their current life. Ahuva, though, had insisted it was quite predictable. "You know, Paul, deep down I've always planned to go home."

"Shall we dance our way to the horizon?" Entropy asked.

Time yielded as he took her in his arms.

They wandered far, dancing through the extensive gardens. Hours, perhaps many nights, had passed.

"It is getting chilly. Shall we return to the house?" Entropy, emboldened, gazed into the eyes of Time.

The many-windowed mansion stood in the distance at the end of a broad gravel path.

"Yes. And I know a shortcut." Time led him sideways through the tall evergreen maze.

"But darling, this route seems most confusing and indirect. We should have taken the straight path."

"Why, you are not so clever as I thought. A straight line is never the shortest path. Look!"

And instantly they were standing on the portico of the château.

"Shall we go in?" Entropy whispered.

"Let us wait and watch the sunrise!"

During the last intense months of her government's negotiations on the disposition of the territories, Ahuva desperately tried to preserve and protect the settlement by invoking the very collaboration of nature. She wrote an article for *Natural History,* which they hurried into publication after she promised she would write them a new essay on the creation of space and matter.

"The red-crested Solomon hoopoe (*Upupa solomonis*), said to have carried the king's invitation to the Queen of Sheba, has not been sighted in this century and had been thought to be extinct. In the last six months, three nests have been spotted within the sector of the settlement Tuval. It is as if time turned backward and sought out history, turning evolution on its head. The distinguished ornithologist Monsieur Verun visited the wilderness, and he has concurred in the finding and even spotted an additional nest on an isolated butte."

Ahuva had engaged a well-known photographer. There were pictures of the surrounding barren desert transformed into gold and orange tones from the setting sun, telephotos of jagged cliffs, and a close-up of an exotic nest filled with the faint, pink-striped heads of fledglings and the white-feathered body and the glorious red crest of the adult bird.

The week the article came out, Ahuva called to read to me from the editorial page of the governing party's paper. "If some pigeons appear in Dr. Adayim's settlement of Tuval it's a miracle. Yes, patriotic citizens, if you're looking for miracles you will find them splattered under every tree branch!"

"What idiots!" Ahuva said. "And speaking of trees. You should see, the new ones we put in the orchards have been growing a foot a month. Another miracle for you." Then the tone of her voice changed, lowered. "But, Paul, that is really all meaningless to me, I admit. My father said miracles are tied to place and time, and only intuition can guide us, though it is a ruthless guide. And I am waiting—here, now—for Nona's miracle. That's why I need you here. I'm about to go crazy."

"Ahuva, Ahuva. I can't leave just now." I couldn't think of anything else to say. I could never change her mind.

Ahuva called the night Christine died. She had seen it on the satellite news. The announcement of Christine's death came among reports of three cases of polymerase dementia appearing for the first time in Western Europe and one case each in Chile and Australia. Though these numbers were still small, it was a sinister turn of events.

"Oh, I'm really sorry about your patient, Paul. Will you come now?"

I kept clearing my throat. I had to think for a moment. Ahuva said, "Things are really accelerating here—out of control. And Nona—Paul, are you there? Will you come?"

"Yes. Yes."

The next morning I found Schpizhof calmly writing at his desk.

"I have to fill out this report for the investigational review panel. Just a formality. Tragic. Tragic. But we did our best."

"I'll be gone for a while. I don't know how long."

Dr. Schpizhof looked up from his desk. I felt a little better thinking that it was Schpizhof himself who had performed the spinal puncture and injected the reverse polymerase. I told myself it was Schpizhof who had made the decisions, who had taken over, taken control. Even so, I knew I would have to get more involved; new cases were being reported. I thought Schpizhof might be angry. He gave me a queer look as if he had figured out what I was thinking.

He stood up from his chair. "Yes, yes, Paul, take off for a while, you deserve it, you look tired, see your wife perhaps." This suddenly made me suspect that Ahuva had been in contact with him, since I had never discussed my personal life with him. "Take off for a while and then come back. You must come back soon, though. You must not look at this unfortunate episode as a failure. It *did* work. We just have to iron out some details."

"Details?"

"Paul, our work isn't finished. You are needed. Time, I'm afraid, is not on our side."

In the evening paper, waiting at the airline gate, I read Christine's father's statement to the Parliament: "My wife and I stand behind these brave and fearless pioneers! They are on the right track. Perhaps soon they will find the answers and Christine's trials will not have been in vain."

Just before dawn Entropy began to fade. He stood on the portico in his usual melancholy manner, seemingly unaware. A sheer opal mist of atoms with their accompanying energies spiraled out from him and wove their way across the garden. The dissolution seemed to occur simultaneously throughout all depths of his body so that with the dawn light, Entropy took on a translucent quality.

"My darling." Time's stretched-out arm glided through Entropy's rarefied substance. "Now that I have fallen in love, you are leaving."

"Don't be sad, my love. For now I will be everywhere." And he smiled as he vanished, for at last he had captured the secret heart of Time.

I had taken fifteen milligrams of Valium when I boarded the flight, hoping I might sleep. But I remained awake, more anxious than ever. Then it was morning, the ocean calm and endless below us.

"All miracles derive from natural phenomena. If you are thirsty, remember even the hardest stone contains water. Moses knew that."

Ahuva was being quoted in an article in *Maclean's* that I read on the plane: "Noted Physicist Battles Her Government's Policy of Territorial Exchange." The settlement of Tuval, the article explained, was now scheduled for dismantling so as not to leave behind anything useful. The settlers were permitted to bring all they could back into the country, and what remained, the standing structures, would all be destroyed. The government would cede territory but not the homes, the buildings, the living town the settlers had created. "We will return the land as we found it, desolate, inhospitable; not on a silver platter," the Prime Minister announced.

Ahuva was frantically trying to publicize the settlers' plight, and she was very good at it.

"Our movement's not, as our critics from various quarters might erroneously suppose, based on religion alone, or geopolitics, but on more fundamental criteria, the evolving universe, the mystery of Time, and the structure of the human heart. We do not define ourselves on religious principles or rituals or remembered history or myth, though we may not discard them either, but rather on that which comes to all peoples from the air, which in our time has become considerably denser, or from water, which in our time has become more exceedingly electric, or from natural, borderless forces, wind, dew, the tropism of plants."

There was an aerial picture of the settlement with its rows and rows of white, boxlike houses, a slope on the side of the plateau dotted with white turbines, and irregular patterns of orchards and fields of commercial flowers.

"On a more personal level, Dr. Adayim, what made you leave your career in Canada so abruptly?"

"This is my home. I belong here and have come to rebuild my life."

"And your husband?"

"He plans to join me."

"Chicken or pasta?" the steward interrupted.

Ahuva was waiting for me in the crowd outside the terminal. She wore a green dress the color of her eyes. Her black hair was topped by a tall white silk toque like a marquise's. People were coming over to her and nodding respectfully.

Ahuva would smile in return. She saw me and waved. As I approached, the air rising from the pavement in front of her trembled in the immense heat.

"You look like a mirage," I said, reaching out my hand to touch her watery image.

"I feel like a mirage!" She passed her hand around her face, pretending she was incorporeal. "It's the hottest day on record, even for here. The wind has stopped. Nature is displeased." Ahuva now put out her hand to demonstrate the absent breeze. She embraced me. "Anyway, how was your trip? I'm sorry about your reverse polymerase. We hear there are new cases in Europe. Just this morning I heard a news report— there may be a case in the capital. There is no such thing as a closed system, and now everything is affecting everything else. Anyway, I'm glad to see you. You could do your research here, you know. I could arrange it."

"I thought there was going to be no 'here' here, if you mean the settlement."

"Time will tell. We'll have to hurry back."

We found her car in the airport parking lot. We drove along the dusty, palm-lined exit road onto the highway. Ahuva kept the windows open because the air-conditioning didn't work. Air was blowing hot and noisy into my face, because she was driving so fast. I had to lean toward her to hear.

"Paul, I wouldn't have left the settlement for a minute for anyone but you. They've already begun taking it apart. They blew up thirty evacuated houses yesterday, then smoothed over the debris with a bulldozer. After today they won't let anyone enter the settlement, only exit. They're trying to coax all the remaining settlers to leave peacefully. Well, you certainly have come at the last minute. Nona's looking forward to seeing you."

"Looking forward?"

Ahuva didn't respond.

"By the way, Ahuva, could you slow down?"

"Paul, I'm not driving fast. And you know very well, Paul, I'm an excellent driver."

Most of the trip I kept my eyes closed because her speeding made me nervous. Soon the roads were narrow and winding. We finally ascended the green mountainous spine that separated the central plains from the territories. I was feeling nauseated and leaned back against the seat.

"Look! Oh, my God, I can't stand it!" Ahuva started crying but didn't slow down. We had come to the last hill on the ridge that looked out over the rugged, amber valley of the wilderness. I was startled to see an endless procession of trees, tiny in the distance, snaking for miles along the winding road in a cortege of flatbed trucks. One could see the brilliant flecks of orange and yellow-green fruit stuck to the trees like sparkles, and here and there thin young desert pines and gnarled acacia trees. They glided slowly in a caravan that stretched out of sight beyond a vast rock formation. We descended into the valley and soon were traveling alongside them in the opposite direction. The proud and leafy captives seemed to shun us. Their roots were tied up with earth in bulging burlap sackcloth. Up close, their colors fluoresced in the intense light. Ahuva had not stopped crying. "They're taking them to be replanted . . .

in the central plains, but they'll never survive. How can you uproot trees in the middle of the dry summer and expect them to live again? They flourished on faith and now . . ."

I closed my eyes again, wishing I had not made this journey. This is all too trying, I thought to myself. The heat, the trailing half-life of Valium, the bizarre cortege, Ahuva's erratic driving—all made me dizzy, nauseated. I wondered which protein, what complex sugarcoated neurotransmitter, what array of synapses was mediating this feeling.

We passed through a checkpoint upon entering the sector of the settlement of Tuval. "Hot! Hot!" the soldier said smiling, waving us through. A low, broad plateau loomed before us, a great pink-gold dish in the late-afternoon sun.

"Paul, are you still sleeping? Look there." Ahuva pointed. Layered out in rows along the northwest slope were white concrete platforms, the stumps, I realized even before Ahuva explained, of the dismantled wind turbines we had seen for the first time on television back in Toronto.

"Even the kabbalists knew," Ahuva said very softly, "we are all interchangeable with energy."

We next approached the settlement gates at the base of the plateau. Another army guard peered in Ahuva's window, then waved us through. Ahuva gave me a tour as we drove the long circular ascent to the settlement. "Not that there's much to see anymore, Paul."

Spread out at the southern base of Tuval's plateau were acres of white plastic webbing under which one could see the muted reds, purples, and oranges of carnations, dwarf roses, frangipani, snapdragons, and hyacinths grown for export. There was a paradisal fragrance in the air. "They didn't take any of this away. It wasn't worth it. They will leave a little for our enemies. But it is an amazing project. Only the minimal amount of water is used, distributed by a fine underground web of tubing."

She pointed below to the "water house," also at the southern base and protected by high concrete walls, whose huge bore, "over three hundred feet deep," tapped into a desert aquifer. "This aquifer connects to the one that supplies the capital, but we use it very sparingly. Tomorrow the government will destroy the water house, closing off . . ." Ahuva suddenly stopped the car and looked at me. "I know what you did wrong.

"It just came to me, Paul—in regard to your reverse polymerase, that is. What you didn't take into consideration—and might in the future, since you must go back to your work, hopefully here—are the effects of third forces. Equilibrium effects in water systems. Maybe you worked under the illusion of a closed system; no system is closed unto itself. Don't you see?"

"I'm well aware of that. That's a fundamental problem in all science. So what is your point? We cannot take into account third forces we don't know about."

"That's true. I was just thinking."

We drove through the settlement, past the rectangular foundations where various buildings once stood, past piles of rubble heaped by bulldozers. Scattered here and there were lone houses, small white boxlike structures whose occupants were still determined to outlast the siege. The doors were locked, the tiny windows shuttered.

"Ahuva, maybe you should leave, it doesn't seem like there's much left. What's the point?"

Ahuva answered calmly. "Oh, are you now a representative of the government? Ninety percent of the people have left, but the rest, the remnant, have stayed and will stay till the end. We won't give up. They'll have to kill us and they won't do that. The country is already on edge. If any of us is hurt, the government will fall."

She turned to me and smiled appeasingly. She took hold of my hand. "I'm glad you came, Paul." And I thought, How beautiful she can be.

"Maybe," she said softly, cautiously, "I can stop this madness. But it will take another miracle, I know. The Prime Minister wants no violence. You think it's already over, so do most of the settlers, but the houses can always be rebuilt, the turbines brought back, the trees replanted. And maybe you could do your research here, set up a lab. We settlers are not dreamy fools. We believe that we can send out all sorts of messages from this place. The more varied we are, the more likely we are to succeed. At least in those areas that are the fruit of man's spirit. What do you say?"

What could I say to all that but "Well, we'll see. We'll see."

Nona was lying on the floor of the kitchen, her spindly legs sticking straight up. She was listening to jazz on a cassette player, her head turning back and forth in rhythm. A woman, Michal, a neighbor of Ahuva's who had been babysitting while Ahuva picked me up at the airport, told Ahuva she was leaving the settlement that evening. "I'm sorry," she was saying, "but it all seems useless now. Perhaps our time will come again." Ahuva smoothed Michal's dark hair, kissed her, and wished her well.

Meanwhile Nona, who was oblivious to all else that was going on around her, did not notice me or Ahuva. But I watched her with curiosity. I felt as if I had forgotten how she looked and if I turned away I would not be able to conjure up the details of her pretty little face.

"Ahuva, she looks just like you." And I thought to myself that I should not bear so much of the blame.

"Yes, but she's still your daughter."

Nona suddenly got up and went into the living room. The same melody I heard on the cassette was now coming from the living room. The same rhythm, the same improvisations, but on the piano.

Ahuva ran out of the kitchen. "'Moonglow'!"

I followed her.

Ahuva stood gaping in the small living room. Nona was sitting at the piano, dwarfed by the spinet, staring intently at the keys, playing, and playing incredibly, for the first time.

"'Moonglow'! She's playing 'Moonglow'! I never played jazz for her before, only classical. Oh, all that wasted time. That was Michal's tape. Michal's jazz. I've always hated jazz!" Ahuva took my hand. "We should be very quiet."

Ahuva and I sat on the sofa, in wonder, watching Nona long

into the night as she played "Moonglow" over and over. She played it all night while the last trees were trundled away under the stars. She played it all night while the army sealed off, one by one, the homes of the vanishing settlers, the diminishing remnant who were already giving up, and prepared the buildings for demolition. And I finally fell asleep as over and over she played, until dawn turned the ground around Ahuva's house a brilliant orange. Lying there on the sofa, I managed to sleep better than I had in a long time, although the music and the sound of explosions invaded my dreams. When I awoke, Ahuva was gone. I went into the bathroom and found the water shut off. Ahuva had filled the bathtub and all her pots and pans with water. There was no electricity.

Light was streaming in the skylight of the house, and through it I saw Ahuva moving on the roof, watching in dismay as the soldiers began surrounding the last houses, imploring the settlers to give up and leave their homes. For a moment she looked down at me through the skylight, smiled nervously, and waved, then there was a commotion, some voices, and she looked away.

Ahuva began shouting, "My daughter and husband are still inside. We are not going." Nona stopped playing the piano and stared up through the skylight. I looked outside through the small living room window. Television cameras were set up in the square in front of the house. The cameramen shouted questions up at Ahuva.

"And what will you do when the army comes for you?"

"I will not leave."

"There doesn't seem to be anything left of your settlement."

"That's an illusion of entropy, assuming there is no symmetry in time. To keep our world alive, we need, we absolutely must, reduce the entropy within history."

The cameramen gave each other funny looks.

I came out of the house and made my way toward the cameramen, waving my arms. "Enough already, enough!"

"It's okay, Paul," Ahuva called out from the roof. "Let them ask questions. Let them observe events."

I began feeling light-headed in the intense morning heat. Music floated from the house. Nona was again playing "Moonglow."

I turned around and went back toward the house. Its simple white exterior was plain and sad. The living room, as I entered, seemed to have gotten even smaller in the few moments I was outside in the glaring morning sun. Nona's little figure leaned forward, expressionless, staring at the piano keys as she played. I was about to touch her shoulder but held back, not knowing how she might react.

I whispered, expecting her to ignore me. "Nona, you have to come with me now. I'm your daddy." Slowly she looked ahead and got up from the piano, gradually releasing the keys of the last chord. Silently, she followed me outside.

The Prime Minister himself had just arrived with a heavily armed entourage to talk to Ahuva and the half-dozen or so settler families who still held out on their own rooftops, humming, defiant, now chanting, "No, no, we shall never leave. No, no, we shall never leave."

"We respect your beliefs, Dr. Adayim," the Prime Minister

pronounced through a bullhorn, "but the country has chosen a different path. Please, leave peacefully."

Meanwhile, several groups of soldiers were climbing up to the other roofs and carrying away the settlers, who offered no physical resistance. Some cried, as their bodies went limp. "Let it be remembered that we did not go willingly." To the army's annoyance the pool of reporters remained, watching, taking pictures. The government, which was trying to keep things calm, had promised that the press could stay until the last settler left. They were, however, limited to the area in front of Ahuva's house to protect them from the explosions and the bulldozers.

Ahuva was still on her roof. She shouted to the Prime Minister, "You have not chosen a path, you have chosen Chaos!" She pointed toward a house that was being demolished.

I called up to get her attention. She looked down and appeared startled.

"Ahuva, look, I have Nona. She came by herself. I asked her to come with me and she listened. Are *you* listening? Nona *listened* and followed me. Now you must come down."

"I'm coming down then," I thought I heard Ahuva say as she lifted the trapdoor on the roof. As she descended into the house she let the trapdoor fall. That's when, as I stood before the house with Nona, I heard an explosion.

I looked up and in terror saw Ahuva rising through the air. I felt myself rising, too, watching. The noise of the explosion made me dizzy. I am still dizzy from it. I will never get over the sight of Ahuva ascending. I see her now, slowly floating up, still in my line of vision. Her dress billows in the warm current above the wilderness. One of her shoes falls off through the air and lands with a thunderous clap on the rubble-strewn earth. Her distant face is now a small dark knot beneath her toque. Ahuva flying, buoyant, as if at sea, borne on the waves of warm air that rise above the wilderness. Borne up at last by waves of miracles and hope.

And then I see Ahuva standing next to me looking very concerned. "What's the matter, Paul? Something's wrong. What are you looking at? Oh, God, what's wrong with your eyes?" And I hear her saying to the small crowd around us, to the Prime Minister, to the group of reporters, "We're going now. My husband says I must go. It's too late. I've lost. It's all over. Come on. Let's go. I cannot bear it." And then to me. "What's wrong, Paul? What's wrong? Let's get away from here."

Behind us several soldiers are carrying whatever they can out of Ahuva's house, her sofa, the piano, which is instantly covered with dust. Piles of clothing, books, including a copy of the *Dialogues,* its pages fluttering in a sudden breeze, are all quickly dumped into large cartons and loaded on a truck. The engineering corps is wiring the house for demolition.

"Oh, dear God. Paul, are you are all right? Oh, your eyes! Your eyes!"

I can see her, feel her warm breath on my face. She is holding me. But she seems to fade away, to blur.

I feel I still know her, and yet I cannot imagine her face or hold on to her. She hovers with me in that small and lonely space, which is all the place I have ever known.

Who is she, after all, I cannot help thinking, though I know she has been so much to me. Who are you, my beloved? Who are you? Oh, yes. Of course. Oh, yes, I think I know. I think I know.

ACKNOWLEDGMENTS

These stories were written over the course of many years. Support and inspiration have appeared in many blessed ways: Pedro de Armas-Kendall, Laura Furman, Richard Howard, Mary Jurisson, Alistair MacLeod, the late W. O. Mitchell, Orlando Rodriguez, and Lois Rosenthal.

Special thanks to my wonderful agent, Nina Ryan, and to my outstanding editor, Celina Spiegel, for their wisdom and friendship.